THE TROUBLE WITH GRACIE

KARY JANE HUTTO

This book is dedicated to anyone who reads it! My hope is that you'll learn a little something about how to become an independent and strong human, and understand that you do not need to rely on someone else to bring you happiness and success in your life, but that YOU ARE that person to rely on to bring yourself joy. Also, I hope you'll be open to the awesomeness and benefits of talk therapy. It's changed me and helped me tremendously.

CONTENTS

A NOTE FROM THE AUTHOR

BE STRONG. BE YOU. BELIEVE IN YOURSELF, and I hope you'll always try and LEARN new things throughout your life!!
  ~Kary Jane Hutto

1

——————

AUGUST

"OH M. GOODNESS! You're so TAN, Gracie! How long were you in Hawaii for, like two months?" Brooke gives me a once-over.

"Dramatic much?" I roll my eyes at Brooke as we walk down the hallway together, past the lockers (yes, we have lockers now!) and toward the open cafeteria doors.

Our senior year officially started this morning. And yes, you read that correctly!

Blondie—aka Brooke—and I are *friends*. Honest to goodness, friends! She and Justin have been steadily going out together since she woke from her coma.

Brooke was in a terrible car crash just before the end of our junior year, but she's completely healed and looking as gorgeous as ever.

She has new clothes for a new school year. Her long, luxurious hair is even more blonde—if that's possible—and she dares to comment on MY tan?!

"Uh, hello? I think you're at least three shades darker than I am." I give her a smirk.

"I know, right? Doesn't my skin look amazing?" Brooke bats her long, lush eyelashes at me. If it had been at the beginning of last year, I would:

1

a) Never would have been walking with Brooke because she'd been such a mean girl to me last year. It was literally awful.

But since she came out of her coma, she had a change of heart. An actual reverse from mean girl to nice friend! It's much, much better to have Brooke as a friend instead of a frenemy.

b) I would have been extremely annoyed by this comment because I have little patience for unnecessary, frivolous, and overly dramatic behavior and comments.

My no-nonsense persona kicks right in, and I just can't help myself. I get so annoyed. I usually keep that annoyance to myself, but last year, Brooke made me crazy from the day she walked into my English class!

She was such a Malibu-tanned, ditzy, flirt, and just plain mean and competitive. I've never been so glad to have that all behind us both. Phew!

But this year? This year is a clean slate, a new beginning. I couldn't care less what Brooke says about herself or her beauty, because I actually got to know Brooke as a real person.

I was pleasantly surprised to find out that she isn't a total blonde bimbo girl at all, that this is all an act, and that she's super smart and actually is a totally caring and fun person.

Shocker, I know, but while Brooke was in her coma, Jake and I ended up visiting her from that awful night she was brought in by ambulance to the hospital, until she awoke about a month later, like Sleeping Beauty from her 100-year slumber.

So here I am, in my senior year, with my new best friend, Brooke, and still dating the most fabulous person, Jake, who gets along famously with Brooke's boyfriend, Justin, also one of my besties. I should be totally happy, right? Right! And I am, but I've got this thought that won't get out of my mind, like ever, that started creeping up just before school started: WILL JAKE AND I STILL BE TOGETHER AFTER GRADUATION?

I know, I KNOW!! I've got a year to figure this out, okay, well, not really a year, I've got a few months to try and talk with Jake about this, see if he's even stressing out as much as I AM about this whole question. Come September, all of us seniors start applying to colleges, writing admission essays, and filling out admission applications online. I literally can't even think about that one bit, because all I can think about is JAKE and ME!

We're entering the cafeteria for my first lunch of the year, the first day of our senior year. And what about my bestie, Clara?

Yeah, we just had a natural and amicable separation, as the guy she's dating hangs out with another group—all great kids, thankfully. Though Clara and I still text here and there, so that's a win-win.

Anyway, back to today, right now, lunch time! Brooke sees Justin and Jake.

They've saved a table, the table that would become our table throughout the year.

We walk over—well, more like aim to not dislocate our elbows on people's heads as we maneuver ourselves around so many teens!

This lunch period is a combo, like all the others, or freshmen to seniors, so there are a lot of kids swarming around!

Luckily, Jake, Justin, Brooke, and I have the same lunch period. Phew! Boy, am I glad! And, as luck would have it, both Jake's sister, Meg, and my sister, Beth.

Beth and I are in the same lunch period, even though we're freshmen. Obviously, both girls are so stoked to have the same lunch period!

And, another cool thing was that even before Jake and I started dating last year, Beth and Meg had become fast friends! It was a cool connection for us all.

Brooke and I squeeze into the table, and I immediately snuggle in close to Jake.

"Hey you! How were your first few classes?" I ask him.

"Really good actually, 'cause if I'm going to have a full schedule this year, I want to learn and not waste any time! I've got Spanish— sorry, we couldn't get the same class this year." Jake gives me a wink as he says this. "Then, American History, and English."

Jake smiles at me with his beautiful smile as he tells me about his classes.

When this boy smiles, my heart goes flip-flop, and my stomach gets butterflies flitting around inside me! Every single time he smiles at me! I hope this never changes! For real.

"Oh my gosh! I love my classes, too. Already! And it's okay about the Spanish class. I love my Spanish class already, and I already know some people, as well as in my art class. I even like my English writing class, so bless up for that!" I smile at him.

He gives me a wee peck on the cheek. I melt inside. *Sighhhh-hhhhhhh.*

We all six talk and shove our food into our mouths as quickly as we can, because lunch period whizzes by! Jake, Justin, Brooke, and I have math together the last period of the day, 'cause this class is a must-take class to graduate.

Calculus—argh! Kill me. Math is the bane of my existence.

At least I am decent at it, as is Justin, but it takes a lot of work for our brain cells, that's for sure! Brooke is actually a whiz at math, as is Jake. So, thankfully, our significant others can help Justin and me.

Oh, Sicily's update: I decided to quit work, as did Jake, by the end of summer.

We've got college admissions to work on, volunteer hours, and maintaining good grades, so we talked with our parents and got the green light to not work during our senior year.

My schedule is very full, and I do not want to mess up my grade point average.

It has been super weird not to work, but having Calculus as a class has already taken a lot of my time.

I cruise through my after-lunch classes: choir, choir for seniors only, a cappella class, my last Science class—Chemistry—and then Calculus.

Wish me luck! These are great classes, but some, such as Chemistry and Calculus, have definitely taken a lot of time to compute in my brain.

The four of us get to walk to the parking lot together every day since we're in Calculus together.

Jake says he'll pick Beth and me up every day and take us home, which is very cool and kind of him. Jake and I will hang out until our sisters join us. It should be a good setup for the year. Beth and Meg join us, and we all pile into Jake's Rubicon and head towards home.

He drops us both off, but before I jump out of the Rubicon, I lean over to kiss him goodbye.

"Thanks, Jake. See you in the morning! I'll text you before I go to bed." I tell him.

"Sounds good. See ya later, Gracie!" Jake says to me with his electric smile.

Beth is already in the house when I arrive and has gone into the kitchen to get a snack. I am always happy when I come home to our cute yellow house, especially since the outside is just as warm as the inside: backpacks flung on the floor, along with various pairs of shoes, and the daily mail strewn on the tiny front entry table.

I, on the other hand, want to talk with my mom about my day. I love to check in with her about everything I'm doing.

Glad we have a good rapport to do this together. This isn't the case for everyone. Like, Jake and Meg's mom is pretty stand-offish.

She's nice, but not a great communicator with her kids. They're both much closer to their dad.

"Hi, Mom!"

Comfy couches with perfectly slouch-worthy pillows, and our house has a certain homey feel and smell, too. Sigh—I love to come home!

There's no answer.

"Mom? Mom!" I am practically yelling now.

"I'm here, sweetheart!" Mom appears out of her favorite spot, her writing lair, popping her head out of the doorway.

"Mom! Hi!" I give my Mom a huge hug.

"Come into my lair, my dear, let's talk about the first day of your last year of High School!" I think I hear a catch in my mom's voice.

I plop into my favorite leather, cushy chair in the corner. It's the chair Dad always sat in, and now I always sit here.

It's full of comfort and happy memories, making me think that my dad is always with me. Which I know he is.

"I have such a great class schedule! I have a very full schedule, but Chem and Calculus will be the only two tough classes. And I have three choir classes! It's like a dream for me!" I smile happily—I love to sing! "And guess what? Jake, Brooke, Justin, Meg, Beth, and I are all in third-period lunch for the entire year! What luck!"

"Wow! That's an incredible schedule and hallelujah! I am so glad Meg and Beth are at lunch together and with y'all. That makes this momma feel better since my baby girl is a freshman this year." She smiles at me, and my mind wanders for a bit.

I never would have thought we'd be where we are today.

Mom is married to none other than her editor, Kenneth Nelsen.

Zac and Sarah are at college together and engaged.

I'm with Jake—it's been almost a year.

It has become a distant memory now that Dad has passed away.

Not that I will ever forget him—duh, that could never happen—just that the pain in my soul heals more and more each day, month, and year.

For this, I am grateful.

"Gracie? Hello?" I realize Mom is talking to me.

"I'm here, sorry, I was just thinking about this past year of GREATS. Kenneth, Jake. Meg. Brooke, and so on. Who knew four years ago we'd be where we are now?"

"Agreed, Gracie. It's like a million Christmas miracles to see how much goodness has occurred in our lives, when we'd suffered such sadness and tragedy."

This time, I definitely hear a catch in Mom's voice. I get up and hug her.

"Soooo, how's the movie production coming? And don't you have to finish two more books?" I ask, changing the subject.

"Ugh, don't remind me," she says, but she grins. My mom loves to write!

"I am actually done with book nine, and then I'll begin writing book ten. The movie production is falling heavily on Kenneth. I am grateful to have him on my side, and as my hubby, because he goes to bat for me and consults me on everything! Literally everything, so that's all I need to have done for this whole crazy adventure into movie-land to come to fruition seamlessly." Mom's smile reaches from ear to ear.

"This is all fantastic! I can't believe this has all happened with your book series! It's like a dream!" I say excitedly.

"It really is, Gracie. About once a day, I have to pinch myself to make sure I know this is all real!" She laughs.

"For sure! I am so proud of you!" I pause before I continue. "So, umm, so I need to ask you something, Mom. Do you have a few minutes to chat?"

"Absolutely! What's up?"

"So, as you know, it's my senior year—I mean obviously, ha-ha—but I've got this thought deep in my brain that keeps coming up more and more, and, um, I know it's dumb..." I don't finish my thought because my Mom interrupts me.

"Gracie, just tell me. Ask away! Please darlin'!"

I take a deep breath. "Okay, okay, so, my question is, WHAT WILL HAPPEN between Jake and me as we start college? Do we do long distance? Do we break up? Do we go to the same college? Should we stay here and attend community college? Argh, I feel like I'm all jumbled up in my brain! Help me!"

I look at my mom, and she's giggling.

"MOM! I'm so serious about this!"

She's still giggling.

"Of course, you are. It just caught me off guard! I really had no idea what you were going to share with me!" She laughs again.

I frown at her.

"Mom! This is a serious thing to me," I say.

"All right, okay, let's talk about this for real. First off, it's still August AND it's your first day back to school. What I'd like to say is that we should discuss this in January—no need for you to freak out needlessly. I mean, aren't things going well between you and Jake?"

"Well, yeah, it's the best. But then I go down a rabbit hole of thoughts and stress, and then more thoughts, and I reach this point without knowing what to do." My eyes fill with tears.

Mom gets up and comes over to me. She lifts me from my chair and envelops me in a nice, warm, momma bear hug.

Then she pulls back and looks straight into my eyes and begins to talk to me.

"You guys are going to know what to do when it comes time to make that decision. I know this is tough right now and seems hopeless and frustrating, but I promise you, things will work out the way they should. Now, what is that right now? No. Do you know what to do right now? Nope. But there's time. Have you and Jake talked about this at all?"

"Somewhat, well, like a little bit. The first decision to make is where I want to go to college. And then talk to Jake about where he wants to apply to college. Then, the next decision is whether Jake and I should go together. Stay here together? Or go to different colleges? I mean, we need to start college apps come October!" I rub my temples.

This subject has been driving me crazy. Argh. It was all too much to think about!

Mom nods thoughtfully. "Okay, so then your first task is for you to decide where you WANT to study, whether Jake will go there or not. Can you do that?"

"Yeah, okay, sure. Sure. But, ya know, that it's not my favorite decision to make, but yeah, I can. I've got a few options.

I'll write down where I want to go and why and share that list with you later on." I start running over them in my head a bit while I'm sitting with my mom.

"Perfect. Tonight, you can write those places out in your journal, too, and then on a piece of paper for me. Then, over the next few days, let's you and I meet up again after school and look up online and see what we need to do for admissions, okay?"

"Okay." I sniffle.

"And, I would suggest that you and Jake talk together. Find out where he would apply with or without you. I know, I know, the whole subject is stressful, but if you guys can get some of your ideas out on paper, then you can breach that tender subject together."

Mom sounds really confident. Which means she knows I can do this and be confident, too.

"Okay, yeah, that does help me. Thank you for talking me through this. I'm going to grab a snack and then go hang out in my room and sort all my binders and syllabi for the semester until dinner time, is that cool?"

"Of course. I think I'll have Kenneth bring home some pizza and salad from Napolitana's, how does that sound?" she asks.

"Fabulous. Thanks, Mom."

I get up from my favorite cozy chair, grab my backpack, and head up to my room.

I feel better now that I've gotten that stress off my mind. It may seem silly to fret about this. But Jake has become such an important person in my life that he's creeping into my future thoughts, too.

Who knew this would happen to me, Gracie? I wouldn't have believed it, but here I am!

The start of my senior year: good friends, an awesome boyfriend, a step-dad, and a heart full of happiness.

2

SUMMER (HAWAII)

As PROMISED, I need to share all the amazing details about our summer trip to Hawaii, the wedding, and everything else!

First of all, Hawaii is magical. Holy cannoli! It's gorgeous. Tropical. Green. Lush.

So many flowers. I mean SO MANY! It was crazy. I took so many pictures! It's like I couldn't even get enough of the beauty around me.

The wedding day for my mom and Kenneth surprisingly brought up some unwanted emotions concerning my dad.

As I've said many times before, my dad is my dad. He's my one and only, and he always will be.

But, having Kenneth in our lives and acting as a father-like figure was needed for all of us more than we knew.

The morning of the wedding, I awoke having had the craziest dream. In this dream, I was sitting on a bench in the park around the corner from our house, talking to my dad. I know, crazy, right?

Well, in this dream, my dad said that Kenneth would hold "his" spot until we see him again one day. He also told me to trust Kenneth and continue to be a great support and someone to talk to for my mom.

I said I would, but I missed him, and although I love Kenneth and am super happy for Mom, I missed him all the time. I started to cry in my dream!

Dad put his arm around me and told me that I might not be able to see him, but that he is always near all of us. He sees what's happening in our lives and loves to see how happy we all are these days. Then he kissed the top of my head and walked away down the pathway, leaving me sobbing!

Then I woke up. Well, that was the best dream ever, and just what I needed, not to be so nervous or sad at all. If Dad was cool with it all, then I was cool with it all.

The day was beautiful and glorious, as every day had been thus far. Our entire trip lasted about two weeks.

The wedding was right in the middle. We did tons and tons of sightseeing before Mom and Kenneth got married.

They had a beach wedding. I can hardly put into words how amazing and romantic it was.

My mom had white and peach, with a soft pink, as her colors and flowers. All the guys had soft pink ties. All the girls were in different styles in light peach.

How did Jake look? UMMM, to die for gorgeous. What about me? Not too shabby.

My hair had grown longer, and I had soft curls at the ends of my hair. It fell nicely around my shoulders.

Zac and Sarah looked so happy and sweet together. Meg and Beth were adorable!

Kenneth has three older kids. They were all there, accompanied by their spouses and children—super nice people.

The ceremony was short and sweet, and then my mom and Kenneth left on their honeymoon, not returning until the next Friday.

Once they'd taken off, we all made plans together. It was ridiculously fun! Kenneth has five grandkids. They're adorable. Jake and I?

We did a lot of kissing throughout this trip. The vibe is so quiet, beautiful, and serene.

Zac and Sarah got engaged!

It was delightful! Zac had preplanned it with all of us. It was

Thursday night of the first week we were there. Zac wanted Mom and Kenneth to see it all, of course, (along with the rest of us).

Zac had told Sarah just before we left for dinner that his stomach was feeling "sickie" (this was just before our luau dinner) and that he might have to use the restroom during dinner, so he was going to scope out where it was right when he got there.

Well, the luau was insanely delicious and so much fun!! Halfway through, Zac excused himself to, in fact, use the restroom.

He was gone for a good ten minutes, but luckily, awesome local dancers were performing, so everyone was distracted.

I was the one to spot Zac out of the corner of my eye, holding an incredible bouquet of tropical flowers.

I quickly glanced at Sarah to make sure she didn't see him. She was so enthralled in the program that she saw nada.

The performance ended, and all of a sudden, we saw Zac standing up in front of us (it was a private barbecue for just our families), and then he took Sarah by the hand and escorted her to stand beside him.

Then, he handed her the bouquet and asked her to look at the flowers for a surprise. Sarah saw a little blue box (a Tiffany's blue box) and opened it up!

Zac took the box, went down on his knee, and asked her to marry him! She squealed and said yes! Zac put the ring on her left hand.

GORGEOUS. A princess-cut diamond, and it was a good-sized diamond. Then, there was a lot of kissing, hugging, and even some happy tears.

Kenneth had been on video duty, so he got it all to send to Sarah's family.

Zac is pretty traditional, so he did get Sarah's dad's blessing before the trip to Hawaii, which I thought was pretty cool.

Later that night, as we were all visiting, a few of us threw out wedding plan ideas and date questions.

Zac answered and said that they probably wouldn't get married for at least two years, as they wanted to finish their first two years of college and then plan their wedding.

While in Hawaii, both Meg and Beth befriended some local kids and had a lot of fun, too.

I was glad. On the very last evening, Jake and I took a long walk together.

Hand in hand, we wound around and around down this amazing pathway from the top of a hill down to a secluded beach.

We watched the sun go down. It was spectacular. Jake told me he likes me so much, and I told him the same.

And he is the one who told me I don't need to worry about what we'll do when we go to college.

He has some ideas in mind. I am realizing this is what he said right now as I write this down, and phew!

That makes me feel so much better. In fact, I now realize I'm such a goof that I get stressed out, while Jake remains level-headed and keeps me sane and on point.

Anyway, the whole trip was magnificent! Like a literal dream!

3

SEPTEMBER

BEEP BEEP BEEP BEEP BEEP

"Oh, honestly!" I slowly open my eyes. "I literally detest my alarm clock!" I roll out of bed, turn off my blasted alarm, and walk into my bathroom.

Time to get on the get! School is on. It's a good thing I love school. I just hate waking up!

I mean, who likes waking up, except for some cray adults like my mother, but anyway, I don't like it! I'd rather sleep in more!

I have fully revamped my wardrobe again. I have been adding in more sandals, fewer jeans, and more dresses.

And doing more things with my hair—Brooke has been teaching me. I know, I know, don't even say it! I'm NOT conforming. Just expanding my options is all. I promise! I remain the same—casual, friendly, and happy to be myself.

Dressed in a yellow, linen knee-length dress and new dark brown sandals, I bounce down the stairs, ready to make and eat my breakfast and pack my lunch.

Jake picks me and Beth up every day, so that's a huge plus.

"Beth, Beetthh, are you ready?" I yell up the stairs to her.

"I'm coming, I'm coming! Outfit trauma this morning. Ugh. High school is SO stressful!" Beth looks exasperated as she arrives in the kitchen.

"Want to borrow something from my closet, sis?" I offer.

She thinks about it for a second. "No, I'm okay for today, but maybe for a few outfits this week?"

"Of course! Never a problem, Beth, never." I smile at her. "Come on, grab your lunch stuff, I've got it ready for you, and here's our breakfast. Jake says he's on his way. Five minutes."

"Okay, cool, cool. Where's Mom?" Beth asks.

"She and Kenneth had an early meeting this morning!"

"Dang, this movie stuff is something, isn't it? I can't believe all that has happened in Mom's life, and our lives! Right? It's amazing." Beth smiles warmly at me.

"For real! I am sometimes in shock when I stop and think about what Mom and Kenneth are working on these days. It's so, well, WOW."

We continue chatting while we pack our backpacks, and my mind wanders off.

My thoughts swirl around in my brain: *Is it really a good idea to leave Beth next year? I don't want her to be lonely. I need to run this idea by Jake.*

I can't talk to him right now, in the car, however, because Beth is right there! Plus, I feel completely distracted anytime he smiles at me! Or winks at me or really LOOKS at me! He's soooo beautiful, and far be it from me to mess up something so good by bringing up something stressful right now.

BUT WHEN? I can't at lunchtime either for the same reason: too many listening ears. So, today, like all the past days since we started school, I paste a smile on my face when I see Jake waiting for me at the cafeteria doors. *Another day, another lunch period!*

We join the others who have already sat down at our regular table.

"Finally, I can eat my lunch! I'm starving, I feel like I never even ate before!" Brooke says dramatically.

I am going to have to work with Brooke on her drama. But of

course, I will help her nicely, like she's helping me with my wardrobe and hair.

"Everyone survive the day so far?" I ask the table in general.

There were various "yeahs" and "sures" from everyone. We all laugh as we get up, clean up, and then take off to our separate hallways.

Jake grabs my hand and gives me a peck on the cheek.

"I feel like I never see you during the day anymore!" he murmurs.

"That's cause you don't, silly," I squeeze his hand, "so that's why we have lunch and study time together after school. In fact, we should all start going to the public library together. Like all six of us! What do you think?"

"Yeah, not a bad idea. It's a lot bigger than any of our family rooms in our homes, that's for sure! Kk. Let's chat after school. Meet you girls by my car then?"

"Absolutely!"

"Bye!" Jake winks at me.

My heart melts.

"Bye!" I give him a little wave.

As I'm negotiating my way through the sea of teens, I end up humming a song.

I can't remember for the life of me what song it is. Dang it! But it reminds me of Jake.

I'll remember. Eventually. Maybe Jake knows? Or Brooke?

Wait! I know what song it is! It's from that awesome new Anime show we watched together called K-POP DEMON HUNTERS.

The lead of a boy band and the lead of a girl band come together, and the whole show reminds me of Jake and me.

And the song they sing together is so incredible, called "FREE".

I continue to hum the song in my head. This be OUR song!

I know I'm dorky. Ha-ha. But I love the words! The music plays in my head until the end of the day.

Good thing I love it. *I will be listening to this on repeat before bed tonight.*

RINGGGGGGGGGGGG

I hurry and pack up so I can get out and into the fresh air!

School days seem so long to me. Sheesh. I exit the back doors to the student parking lot.

I see Meg and Beth coming towards me, surprising me that they made it through the craziness of all of those students so quickly.

"Hey girls!" I wave as soon as Meg and Beth can see me.

"Hey, back!" I hear Beth say.

We always gather at Jake's Rubicon after school, and then we proceed to discuss our days with one another while I scan the parking lot, looking around for Jake.

There he is. He's just so absolutely good-looking. Sheesh. Be still, my heart.

He's walking with Brooke and Justin. Justin usually parks next to us.

As soon as they all reach us, I blurt out my idea about studying at the library.

"So? What do you think, guys?" I await their responses.

I hear "yeahs" and "sures" coming from everyone.

"Okay, so I'm thinking by 4:00 pm we should be good to go to meet up? We don't have to go every day, but I'm thinking at least twice a week?" I say.

Everyone nods in agreement.

"Cool! Fuel up. I've got a bit to do tonight. Anyone else?" I ask everyone.

"Sigh, so much!" Brooke says with obvious exasperation.

"And Brooke, Justin, Gracie, and I have to start looking at filling out our college apps in just a few weeks, so the library will be a good place to do that." Jake smiles.

The smile makes my knees buckle with weakness.

But I've got a lump in my throat because of the thought of leaving Beth when I go to college.

Blast. I hate to have to make so many decisions. It makes my brain cells so jumbled and confused!

"Gracie, you okay?" Jake says to me once we're all in his car.

"Totally. Okay. Yep. All good!" But I am a big, fat liar. It's NOT all good. I'm back to feeling stressed again about my future! And Beth's!

"Okay," he drops his voice. He's not convinced. I can tell.

"Promise!" I feign a smile.

He smirks at me. "Yeah. Nice try, Gracie. We will definitely talk later!"

I just smile again at him and then turn to look out the window.

Fortunately, Beth and Meg are deep in conversation, so they don't even notice our interaction in the front seat, which is good because I don't want Beth to know what I'm thinking. I mean, I know that Beth will have Meg.

But it's not the same. Ya know? It's not like they're sisters and live together. They're just besties!

Jake drops Beth and me off at home so we can get changed and eat some food.

"See ya in a while, Jake!" I yell from my front door, adding a boisterous wave, too.

Beth and I stop into Mom's office. It's now become an after-school ritual for Beth and me these days.

"Mamasita? It's your girls!" I rap on her door softly.

"Come in, my lovelies! Come in!"

Beth and I follow suit, and I scurry to my favorite leather chair. She nabs the bean bag next to me.

"Okay, so spill! How was the day? How will this semester turn out with your classes, you're both in?" Mom asks.

Beth starts off the convo. "I have to say, it's wayyyyy better than I had anticipated. Y'all don't know how very stressed I was going into my Freshman year. Argh. I was terrified!"

"Beth!" Mom and I say in unison.

"Why the heck didn't you say anything to any of us??" Mom scowls a bit as she says this.

"Uh, yeah, ditto. I literally see you every day!! Why didn't you say anything, silly girl??" I add my own scowl as I say this.

"Well, you know, there was Hawaii. The wedding. Zac and Sarah getting engaged; getting them out the door to college; there never was a good time to talk about how I was feeling!" Beth murmurs.

Mom gets up quickly and strides to Beth. She pulls her up and into a momma hug.

She looks directly into Beth's pretty green eyes.

"Ma'am, there is ALWAYS time for you. For you to talk, for Zac, for Gracie. You three are THE most important people in my life. Never forget this." She kisses Beth on the forehead, which is almost at her height.

Beth has grown a lot over the summer, I realize.

My sister plops her backpack down. THWUNK!

"Okay, okay! I'm sorry. Well, anyway, it's good. I love having Meg with me at school. I love eating lunch with all y'all." She waves her hand towards me. "It's made it so GREAT for Meg and me. She's been just as freaked out as I have!"

"Okay, y'all are so fired!" I laugh. "Good grief, child, you both should have said something!!"

"Yeah, I see that now, but anyway, I told you guys now, so we're good?" Beth gives us both a thumbs up.

"Yes, of course," Mom says.

"Sure thing, but sister to sister, you better tell me the MINUTE you're feeling stressed about anything, got it?" I add.

"Yes, ma'am!" Beth grins as she adds a salute.

We continue with some small talk and chat about the school day in general.

I run out and grab some food for us to eat while we visit together.

I don't bother changing, nor does Beth. We'd both rather stay put and visit with our Mom.

PING!

"Jake and Meg are here! Oh! Ha, forgot to share this little tidbit. The six of us are going to start studying at the public library three times a week. Today is one of those days!" I explain.

"Great idea, and sure, of course! Okay, so can y'all be home by 6:30 pm-ish?" Mom asks.

"Yeah, that gives us all a good two hours of uninterrupted study time. Sure. Thanks, Mom! See ya!" I hug her and grab my backpack.

Beth does the same. We head out the door and into Jake's waiting Rubicon.

I'm always grateful he's cool with driving us everywhere.

The library study idea is most successful. Once we arrived, everyone put their phones away and got to work.

I personally got a lot done. I am definitely looking forward to a Wednesday and a Thursday study sesh, too.

With our goodbyes said, Beth, Meg, and I pile into Jake's Rubicon when I suddenly feel like I need to talk to him about some of my thoughts.

The girls start looking at college courses in the catalog that Beth somehow got her hands on. You can take classes at the community college after your sophomore year, so you can start taking some as early as next summer.

So they are occupied and won't hear our discussion. Additionally, the drive time to my house is approximately 15 minutes.

"Um, Jake?" I start tentatively.

"Yes, Gracie?" He turns to me and smiles his beautiful smile. I swear his eyes twinkle when he smiles.

Focus Gracie!

"I've been thinking about a certain sister of mine who will be left behind if I were to go to another city for college, and I just don't know how I feel about this. At first, my main worry was you, of course, but then, the other day, these thoughts came flooding into my mind, and I couldn't believe I had been so selfishly thinking only of myself. What kind of a sister am I? Good gracious." As I finish my thought, I hope Jake will hear me out on this.

Not trying to beat a dead horse, but I'm obviously still doing just that. I stress too much sometimes. I know I do.

Jake doesn't answer immediately.

Which literally freaks me out.

I'm not sure whether I should wait or say something. I decided to stay.

"Gracie, I can see why you're bringing this up—again," Jake's tone is a little brisk, "but we keep talking in circles and aren't making a lot of progress."

I look at him wide-eyed.

"Um, yeah, well, yeah, I just get worried about things, as you know." My voice gets tinier by the end of my sentence.

"Yeah, well, I need to go to the University of Austin. I'm sorry to have to say this to you, Grace, but I'm unable to attend the community college. I'm sorry. I just can't." Jake is facing forward. I can see he's bugged. I need to nip this convo in the bud. And quickly.

"Oh, okay." I fake a little laugh. "Of course you can't. And Beth will be fine. Pfff. No problem at all."

I feel tears prick my eyes. I turn my head to look at the window.

We're almost to our house. I concentrate on the music still playing. It's like watching a movie.

The characters are upset. The music starts quietly, then the volume increases.

I feel the tension between us. I am doing everything I can to quell my emotions and stay calm.

I hope my potential tears dry up immediately.

Jake pulls into our driveway. I waste no time getting out of the car. I grab my backpack.

He doesn't say anything, which isn't like him at all. He just watches me leave.

"Thanks, Jake! Bye Meg! See you both in the morning!" I say and close the passenger side door.

I don't give Jake the opportunity even to say goodbye or anything.

He looks at me. It's kind of a weird look, but I just continue smiling and close the car door.

Beth sidles out, grabs her backpack, and follows me as we walk to our front door.

I turn and wave. And then I open the door and rush to my mom's studio. I'm going to burst if I don't talk to her before dinner.

Beth is oblivious to all of the emotional fireworks going off in my chest and brain.

I knock softly on the door and open it. I dash to "my" chair. I plop down and drop my backpack.

"Umm, Gracie, you okay?" Mom asks me.

"No. I think Jake and I had our first argument in the car just now, coming home from the library."

"Oh dear. What happened?" She gives me her full attention.

"Well." I sniff. "I threw out the idea of both of us maybe staying around here for college, and he got real quiet, then said angrily that he HAD to go to UT Austin for his major. So, I backed off from the subject and faked a smile, and as soon as we were in the driveway, I said goodbye and flew out of the car!" I sniff again and wipe a few tears off my cheeks.

"Well, other than running away when Jake pulled into our driveway, I think you handled that situation pretty well. And now, you're clear on what Jake wants to do for fall," Mom reasons.

"I guess—sheesh! We've never even spoken cross words to one another EVER, so this was some sketchy, new territory that's for sure. Now what do I do?" I give my mom a very pleading look.

"And now the ball is in his court, and you're going to see him tomorrow!" Mom answers me with a contented smile.

"And all these wild and crazy and panicky emotions that are trying to take over my mind and body, what exactly do I do with those??" I give my mom yet another pleading look.

"Yeah, so that part truly sucks. I don't even like to say that word, but that part is literally the worst part of any type of argument or disagreement: the feelings that accompany it." She then walks over to me and pulls me up from the chair.

"Welcome to the exciting world of adulting and relationships." Mom gives me a quick hug. "Would you like to head to your room for a bit or come and eat with us all? Can you suppress your feelings enough to get through dinner?"

I am silent for a bit as I ponder this.

"Yeah, I'm so starving. I think I'd best eat, then I'll go to my room after we eat."

"Okay, let me shut down my laptop, and let's go into the kitchen together. Kenneth is making us homemade pizza tonight, oh, and breadsticks. Can you smell the marvelous aromas?" Mom closes her eyes and inhales deeply. I do the same.

"Holy! That smells insanely good!"

Mom and I walk out together from her studio; she closes her door, and we both head into the kitchen, where Kenneth is busy cooking each pizza one at a time in his home pizza oven, situated on our back patio.

"It smells divine! It's like we're in a legit restaurant! Kenneth—you've outdone yourself!" I say as Mom and I enter the kitchen. Beth is already at the table, eating her pizza that just came out of the pizza oven.

"Wooooowwww!" Beth says with her first bite. "This pizza is incredible. Mmmmmmm."

Oohs and aahhs continue from my mom and me.

Kenneth's cheeks start to pink up with embarrassment.

"Y'all are just being nice." He grins.

"Umm. No. No, we're not! This pizza is so freaking good!" I comment with enthusiasm.

"Well, then, good! We should have a homemade pizza night once a month, maybe?" Kenneth has a wide smile on his happy face, and we all continue to comment with each bite until the pizza, salad, and breadsticks are all eaten.

Stomachs are full. Everyone is visiting contentedly together, and then we all peel off one by one and meander to our different rooms— a perfect way to end my not-so-great Monday.

I take out my journal. It's time for me to get every single feeling out of my soul.

I am glad I was able to enjoy dinner. The pizza was ridiculously good, and the company was too. I begin to write and write and write.

I pour out my whole soul into my journal.

I may have checked my phone like thirty times during dinner—no text from Jake.

Again, it's weird, but I have to let him have some time to himself. I'm just not used to this.

We've spent every minute together, so this is very new and uncomfortable for me.

I add that to my writings. At least 30 minutes pass as I continue writing when I hear a ping on my phone.

I'm afraid to look. If it's Jake, I'm sure he's going to tell me I suck as a girlfriend and that we need to break up.

I'm a nervous wreck. Kk. Here I go. I'm checking my phone!

Jake <I am sorry. I was dumb to treat you badly. I haven't told you this yet, and this isn't an excuse for my behavior, but my parents have been fighting again, just like they did in California, and my mom is acting strangely again, as if she's going to leave, which has put me in fight-or-flight mode.

What kind of boyfriend am I if I don't confide in you? Share how I'm feeling? Instead, I got silent and was mean. I am so very sorry, Grace. You definitely don't deserve that>

I sit still in shock. First of all, I am happy that Jake texted me and apologized.

I mean, look at what he's going through—AGAIN!! I'm sorry for them all, and I'm even sorry for his mom, too. Ugh. I mean, I know firsthand how it feels to have a parent gone.

Still, I can't imagine having my mom live with us, only to leave and then come home and leave again!

And, I'm not trying to be selfish, okay, maybe I was being slightly selfish, and well, I did have a few thoughts that maybe Jake would break up with me.

I got a grip and figured this was just a minor bump in our path and something we could fix easily.

Yeah, I know I'm always dramatic, but dang, that was a weird and uncomfortable drive home.

I reread his text so I can respond to what he's shared with me, but first, I send a text to my mom.

Grace <Jake texted and apologized>

Mom <so glad, sweetie, sleep well>

Grace <thanks for being there for me tonight>

Mom <always>

I'm ready to text Jake back.

I will definitely give him a huge hug tomorrow morning and tell him that I'm so sorry for what's been happening at his home.

Grace <hey Jake, thanks for your text and apology tonight, and let me please apologize too for adding to your stress!>

Jake <no way you could have known about my mom unless I told you>

Grace <k, sure, agreed, but still, this whole sitch tonight is showing me that we can surely work on communicating our feelings better with one another, cool?>

Jake <def and again I'm sorry>

Grace <I'm the one who needs to be sorry for adding extra stress on you—I will chill on the whole community college subject, okay?>

Jake <sure thanks, and I will work on telling you how I'm feeling if I feel like something you're wanting to talk about is getting on my nerves, and ditto for you. I'd better get some rest. Thanks for being my person>

4

———

OCTOBER

TIME FLIES when you're studying all the time! Sheesh.

I feel that's all I do these days. Seasons change.

Ha.

Just kidding, this is Texas. Our fall doesn't even start until some-time in November!

But the seasons in my life are changing towards the end of senior year, and time feels like it's whizzing by me like a strong Texas wind.

I feel both nervous and excited. Who wouldn't?

To finish high school is 1. A YAY, finally, and 2. I will be moving forward with my future life.

I am led to that dreaded topic again: what *will* I be doing next fall?

I've been talking with Mom and Kenneth a lot about it all. Jake and I have discussed it extensively.

The overall decision I've come to is to apply to a few colleges and the community college, and see how I feel when, or if, I receive acceptance letters.

Mom, Jake, and I have also talked together at length about both Beth and Meg being at home "solitas," (alone in Spanish), and well, we're all just unsure.

Mom just wants us both to apply wherever we want to go and then decide.

Jake and I are similar and low-key about which colleges to apply to. Thankfully.

Mom, Kenneth, and Jake's parents (I need you to give y'all an update on Jake's parents, btw—more on that in a minute) have also been talking with Beth and Meg, respectively, about what life will be like next year if Jake and I are gone as well. Sigh.

Okay, update on Jake's parents: Meg told Beth, who then told me, and I confirmed what Beth told me, because I ended up having a talk with Jake today, as he mentioned earlier that their parents are doing worse. This whole situation breaks my heart.

Daphne, Jake's mom, has only been back home with them all for, like, what, just under six months, I guess?

Ugh. Hate this for them. Life is hard enough as a teenager! Let's add in drama, or a family crisis, or any other stressful situation on top of trying to figure out where you fit in this thing called LIFE, and it really throws a huge bump in your path!

I'll keep checking in to see how things are going, fingers crossed that Daphne can work out her personal issues and stay around for good.

My brain is tired. I've started a few college apps and then realized I need wayyyy more volunteer hours. How the heck will I squeeze that in? I need to be superhuman just to fill out my college applications. I need excellent grades. Excellent referrals.

Excellent and legitimate volunteer opportunities and more. I'm going to bed. I'll think about this all in a few days.

Jake and I need a great date day, and we all need a fun family Sunday game day. Thankfully, it's Friday, and we've made it to November.

5

NOVEMBER

"I AM SO STOKED to go on a day-date with Jake!" I say to Beth.

She's sitting on my bed while I'm choosing my outfit. I've gone through about five different choices.

"Okay! You're gonna make me crazy, Gracie! I like any of the 20 dresses you've shown me with a pair of sandals. Just choose already!" Beth cries.

I know she's serious, but in a kind way. She rolls her eyes and giggles at me.

I know. I'm ridiculous. It's not like we haven't been dating for just over a year, cause we sure have!

In fact, today we're celebrating one year together! I suggested going to the bookstore and getting ice cream again, like we did on our very first date.

Jake agreed. Then we will watch a movie and have dinner with Brooke and Justin. What a great day it will be!!

"Fine! I'll wear the berry tiered dress with my brown sandals. What about my hair?" I ask.

"Seriously? You know I'm not like you, sis. You're going to have to ask for backup from Brooke for that info!"

We both laugh. But it's true. Beth is wayyy more chill in her outfits.

Even more than I was. She always looks cute, nice, and clean, of course.

However, she has always been more focused on her classes and earning good grades to start accumulating college credits next year.

She's just so smart!

I get dressed in my berry-colored, tiered knee-length dress, put on my new brown sandals, and then start working on my makeup.

I've been learning to apply my makeup more effectively lately. Not tons, just a simple cover-up, powder, blush, and a toned lip gloss.

I don't wear anything more than a lash primer either. Makes my life nice and simple. I can't handle too much on my face. Ew.

Next, I send a text to Brooke for hair help and to finalize our plans, such as where to meet her and Justin later for dinner and the movie.

Grace <help! What should I do with my hair?>

Brooke <girl please. Simple curls at the bottom of your hair; leave it down. Throw on a headband or a headscarf>

Grace <okay! Done. See you two later on>

Brooke <perf>

As I finish up my hair, a thought comes into my mind: *Jake could get into a college, and I may not.*

Then what? Ohhhh, I don't like where my brain is going with this. Oh no no no. I hadn't even thought of this.

Why am I thinking of this now? Of all the times to have these worrisome thoughts, just before Jake picks me up? Okay, brain enough.

It's a free day. I'm tired of all the college applications and essays, etc. Etc.

I am going out with my adorable boyfriend today, and that's all I need to worry about today!

Here's hoping my speech to myself will stick, haha.

I glance at myself one more time in my mirror. "You've come a long way, Gracie, from a few years ago, but mostly since last year! Thank you, mirror, for being your best girl's confidante!"

I smile at myself, grab my purse and phone, and head downstairs to say goodbye to Mom and Kenneth.

Jake is bringing Meg with him, so Beth has already left my room (since she got bored with my revolving outfit sitch) and is waiting in the kitchen for her.

"Bye guys! I'm heading out. We've got a lot planned today, so I just wanted to make sure you both know I won't be home 'til probs 11 pm. Cool?" I call to Mom and Kenneth.

"Cool with me!" Mom replies.

"Ditto for me!" Kenneth adds.

"Thanks, guys. You're the best!" I wave to them both, turn, and sort of float out of the kitchen.

I love to see my mom happy again. It's the literal best thing ever.

I hear a knock at the door. I reach out to answer it when Beth veers in front of me!

"Okay, crazy. What the??!!" I'm obviously kidding, but why is she in such a rush?

"Meg! Come on in!" Beth scoots me aside. "Bestie entering our home. Move aside, sis."

"Wow. Chill out, little Sis. What gives?" I give her a sneer face, but I'm still mostly kidding.

"Nothing. Just glad to have my friend Meg here since you and Jake are ALWAYS together." Beth says with obvious sarcasm.

"Uh oh. I'm sorry, Beth. You're completely right. Jake and I ARE always together. Would it help if I suggested that Jake and I take you and Meg out for a fun day-date?" I ask.

"Yes please!" Both girls reply in unison.

"Ha ha ha. Alrighty then. How about lunch and shopping next Saturday? Can you hold out for a whole week?" I grin at them.

"I guess," Beth retorts, sounding defeated. But then she perks up when Meg gives her an elbow to the side. "Yep, that sounds good, Gracie. Thanks."

"Are you sure, Beth? I'm not totally convinced you're being completely honest with your big sis." I shake my finger at her.

But Beth gives me a thumbs up and smiles, then looks at Meg. Meg smiles too.

"Okay, yeah. I promise, Gracie, it's cool. Next Saturday. Bye!" Beth says.

And they both run down the hallway and up the staircase to Beth's room.

That girl! She's growing up. This behavior is a new and weird concept for me to wrap my head around. Beth with feelings?

She's maturing rapidly. So, I suppose this is a change as well. Beth and I need to interact more, just the two of us, I guess.

She never used to care. I'm actually both surprised and glad that she cares now. She's always had her nose in a book for years, so to hear her share her true feelings is awesome!

This is also the second time in a few weeks, as the first instance was when she was telling Mom and me about how stressed she's been about starting high school.

None of us had a clue about how she felt! Mom and I felt really bad.

I get lost in thought as I reach out for the passenger-side door handle. I open the door and hop in.

I remember telling Jake a long time ago that waiting for him to open my door was going to make me crazy—my independent streak so obviously shining through—so I released him from doing so anymore.

"Hello, Jake!" I lean towards him and kiss him on his smooth, just-shaven cheek.

"You smell amazing!" I flutter my eyelashes dramatically and fan myself.

"Ha. You're cute! But, like, for real. You actually ARE very cute. Well, adorable really, and you also smell delicious." Jake makes a dramatic eye-rolling gesture to match mine.

We take each other's hands, and Jake puts on our favorite playlist on his Spotify. Then we both settle back in relaxed comfort.

"Okay, so you're cool with the bookstore and ice cream date today? I just discovered a new Independent bookstore called The Book Nook, which has a very independent bookstore vibe that I think you'll love. Oh, and I wanted to see if you're up to try that Korean fish ice cream shop?" Jake says.

"Ahh, you're the best. Yes please! It all sounds amazing. Except for fish ice cream! Ew!" I make a face.

"I was waiting for that reaction from you. The fish are made from a waffle batter and poured into a mold, then fried in extremely hot oil. Fill it with ice cream and Nutella. And then add any topping you'd like!" Jake grins.

"Now that's my kind of fish ice cream!" I gush with excitement.

The bookstore is STELLAR. We both immediately decide upon stepping into the store that it's our new go-to bookstore.

This store has themed walls of books throughout the space. Mysteries Travel. Gardening. Children's books, etc. You name it. They've got it.

Jake and I take our time as we peruse the books for a good hour or more. Jake finds some excellent spy series he's going to try.

I see a collector's copy of *Little Women* and *Emma* for my Regency books collection. I already have *Persuasion* and *Pride and Prejudice* at home, both illustrated by the same artist.

Jake purchases his books. Since we both want to hang onto our hard-earned cash, we talked the other day and decided NOT to buy each other gifts.

So I purchase my books with my own money.

Holding hands as we leave the store, we decide to walk around the shopping center for a bit before going for lunch and then getting our Korean ice cream treat.

"I think we can actually eat somewhere around here. Are you starving?" Jake asks me as we continue to walk hand in hand.

"Yes. Let's find a place to eat here. Please," I beg.

Luckily, we spot a Tex-Mex place we've been wanting to try.

We usually try not to go on many expensive dates—it's a money-saving tactic—but today is a celebration.

Once we sit and place our order, I begin to share my interaction with Beth from earlier today.

"So, she was actually wanting to hang out with me and us. She's never been like that before. Never. I am frankly shocked," I say.

"What did you tell her?" Jake asks quizzically.

"I suggested that you and I could take them out shopping and get some lunch together next Saturday? I didn't make any promises since I just threw that idea out there. What do you think, Jake?"

I start digging into my double-enchilada entrée, with beans and rice, waiting for Jake to answer. The #11 is my fave dish to order.

"Yeah. I'm cool with that. I need to help around the house with some chores and such, since I only applied to the University of Texas at Austin and won't need time this morning to fill out any more apps. My dad isn't cool with this, but I feel confident in my choice. Especially because I found out that UT Austin has a well-known Public Broadcasting major. And yeah, I know that's pretty narrow-minded, but I feel good about my application."

A slight ping of hurt nips at my heart. Jake knows EXACTLY what he wants to study, and the work he wants to do, oh, and where he wants to go.

I don't at all. It is a little frustrating for me. I, of course, will never let on to Jake that I'm feeling frustrated. Or maybe even a tad jealous that Jake has everything so planned out.

No, no, I would never, because that's not fair to him. I try to snap out of my emotional spiral and bring my emotions back under control. Quickly.

"I am so happy for you. That's wonderful. I'm glad you're zeroing in on what you're going to study and where." I give him a gentle smile and continue eating.

I have more to say, so I'll share two more things, then, but I def will ask Jake about his parents.

"I think I'm going to apply to TWU, UT Austin, and our community college. I don't know what to study. Oh! I forgot to tell you! I found a volunteering opportunity for the four of us at our local Food Pantry. We can visit the local food pantry every Tuesday. They need extra volunteers on that day because they receive a large number of food donations. My mom knows the owner there, so ya know. It's who ya know, ya know?" I break out into laughter.

Jake's eyes lit up. "That's incredible. Thank you, Gracie. Well, and thank you to your awesome mother, too. Please tell her thanks from me. I was stressing over that big time."

"Yeah, me too. Phew. I'll tell Brooke and Justin when we see them later today."

I hesitate for a moment.

"Jake?" I say quietly.

"Yes?" He responds softly.

"What's going on at home with your parents?" I hope he's okay with me asking. Don't want to be too intrusive, but I do want to know.

"Not good. The fighting is awful. My mom says she's found a place in California with her best friend. She says she'll be moving out sometime in the spring. I guess. I was hoping they could go to counseling together. Dad will do it. My mom won't. It sucks. But enough about my homelife! We're here to celebrate our one year together." He tries to sound happy, which he surely does not.

"Jake, come on, I care about you. These things are happening in your life right now, so it is important to me too. I mean, how can I best support you and Meg, or what can I do, or my family, to help you guys?"

I smile at him with an eager expression.

"Well, that's actually very kind of you. Remember when I first moved here and we came to dinner a lot, and your mom had Meg over when I wasn't home, or my dad? I think if y'all could help with that, it will keep things as steady and secure as is possible with our situation."

He lowers his head and pushes his rice around his plate, then continues. "Half the time, my mom is never around, and the other half, my parents are fighting or in separate rooms." He grimaces after he shares this.

"Dang, I am sorry. Okay, done! I will talk with my mom and Kenneth tomorrow about it all. And, Jake, thanks for sharing your personal family sitch. I know it's painful." I give him a big smile and take his hand across the table.

"Thank you, Gracie, and, umm," I hear Jake's voice get more serious. "While we are holding hands, I wanted to tell you something. This past year with you has been. Well, terrific. I've never had a girlfriend before you. And I wasn't looking for one after the whole Brooke situation before moving here. But anyway, once I met you, well, I was hooked." My heart does a flip-flop inside me when I hear these sweet words.

He continues. I am gazing into his awesomely blue eyes—my fave feature of his.

"I know this college stuff is stressful for both of us. But no matter what, we will be together. You make me happy. You're pure sunshine in my life. You came into my life when I needed it, with my mom being gone and all that. Anyway, things will work out with college and my parents, as well as it can—and I'm hoping we both get into UT Austin."

Tears gather in the corners of my eyes. His words penetrate my entire soul. "Well, those are just the nicest things to say to me ever. Thank you. And you know how I feel! You're the best thing that's ever happened to me. I didn't think I'd ever have a boyfriend, ever! I hope for sure you get into UT Austin. Not sure about my application to them, but we'll see. For now, I'm so happy we can be together. It makes me happy every day, too." I feel my eyes tear up.

"I've got a gift for you, Grace." Jake smiles.

"What? I thought we decided no gifts!" I protest.

"We did, but I found this for you and couldn't resist." Jake pulls out a necklace box. He pushes it across our table over to me.

"Jake!" I whisper his name and tilt my head at him to say WHAT and WHY.

"Just open it, silly." He chuckles.

"Okay, but you shouldn't have." I open the box to find a beautiful silver necklace with a heart pendant and my name engraved on it.

"Ohhhh, myyyy, oh, wow, I love it!" I exclaim.

"Turn the heart over," Jake says to me softly.

I slowly turn the heart over. It has Jake inscribed on the back side of the heart.

"Jake . . ." I look back up at him and into his eyes.

He then rises to come over to my side of the booth and puts the necklace on me, then pulls me up into a hug.

"Thank you," I whisper sweetly into his ear. "You are an amazing human."

We stand hugging each other for a few minutes until our server comes to our table with the bill. We both take our seats awkwardly.

Jake puts his debit card in the bill tray and hands it back to the server. As he walks away, we giggle quietly.

"Wow, that was so awkward and embarrassing!" I laugh.

"Completely—sheesh. Well, once Marco comes back, we need to get going if we're going to make it to get our fish ice cream and then meet Brooke and Justin first for dinner, before the movie later tonight."

Our server brings the bill tray back. Jake signs it, puts his debit card away, and we both get up and walk out.

Jake grabs my hand. I lean myself onto his strong shoulder.

"Thanks for a great day-date, Jake," I say in a soft but sweet tone.

"You're very welcome." I lift my head and turn to look at him.

He gives me a warm smile and squeezes my hand as we walk out of the restaurant to his Rubicon.

We pull up and park right outside the fish ice cream store called, "Delish Fish," and see that it's already packed with happy people ordering and eating.

"Wow! The 'Delish Fish' must be a pretty popular treat choice," I say as I jump down out of the Rubicon.

"Yeah, I had no idea. Glad we decided to try it, though. It looks like the line is moving pretty quickly. Oh! I can see through the window that they've got ordering kiosks. That's helpful," Jake replies as he takes my hand and leads us inside "Delish Fish."

Jake and I head towards the kiosk.

"Holy! There are way more choices than I thought there would be. How can I decide?" I laugh.

"Yeah, way more. How about this five-pack deal? Then we can have a variety of choices. One will be a Nutella-filled waffle fish topped with ice cream. Another is custard filled with a topping. Another is Matcha custard with a topping, then we can repeat any of those," he reads.

"Um, yes please. Can we double the Nutella one and the custard one, please?" I implore.

Jake laughs at me. "Of course."

He places our order, and within 15 minutes, we're holding a warm box of "Delish Fish" treats!

There are a few benches outside that we gravitate to, where we sit and start tasting and sharing the waffle fish treats.

Suddenly, Brooke bounds right up to us. "Oh my gosh!!!! I adore your necklace!! Gracie, it's just gorgeous. Jake! Nice job." She punches him in his upper arm.

"Thanks, Brooke. Appreciate your approval." Jake smirks.

"I know! I loveeee it! I was so surprised. Jake's the sweetest," I gush.

I grab his hand and we four continue to walk to our seats in the theater. For some reason, I suddenly remember the first time Brooke swindled her way into my plans that one Saturday.

Super glad we're way past that nowadays! Thankfully.

"Hey, you two, tell us about the fish ice cream place? Did you end up going?" Brooke asks us both.

"Oh yeah, we did after we went to eat. It was delicious. You and Justin seriously need to go check it out. I had Nutella at the bottom, followed by ice cream, and then Oreo sprinkles on top. It was divine." I tell Brooke.

The movie we're seeing is the final movie of one of our favorite action movie series.

We love a good action movie. Throughout the film, though, fleeting thoughts shoot in and out of my mind: *Can I actually get into UT Austin? Do I have the grades? Would the volunteer hours help? What if I didn't get in? Then what?*

I try super hard to suppress these thoughts. I am not doing a great job. I keep trying.

Around 6:15 pm, our movie ends. We loved it! The four of us discuss the awesomeness of it as we walk to the guys' cars.

"Okay, so let's go to Gloria's? Has anyone eaten here before? I've heard it's not Tex-Mex at all. It's Argentine food, which I heard is yummy from my parents. Is that okay with y'all?" Brooke asks us all. I hear she uses the word "y'all." She's getting a little Texan on her!

We all agree.

However, all through dinner, I am fretting on the inside. STILL.

Calm down. Gracie, there is no need to stress about something that hasn't even happened yet. Calm down.

I continue to talk to myself in my brain throughout dinner. Smiling and laughing at the conversations. By the end of the dinner, I had finally put away my worries enough to be able to enjoy the rest of the evening. Jake takes me home, and I thank him again for the necklace before we share a sweet goodnight kiss.

I need to therapize—talk to my mirror about this.

And I will have to stop fighting myself about this all, because it is going to drive me absolutely crazy. And actually, it's time to start my journal.

My therapist has suggested it multiple times.

Tonight seems as good as any night to start. *Sorry, cute mirror. Time to really get down to business and clear my brain AGAIN of all of these thoughts that are driving me crazy. I know I've written stuff out before, but man oh man, I need to write it again and again until I chill out for good. I know I can do this!!*

There is no need for me to worry about something that has not even happened yet.

Or might ever occur. But even if it were to happen, I would need to have an emotional game plan in place.

It's what I've already thought about.

I just need to get my generals done while I figure out what I want to do.

And, since Beth's feelings have begun to reveal themselves, I am leaning towards staying around.

I am trying to be brave and think about both situations: going away or staying home while Jake goes away. What would that look like?

How would I feel? How would Jake feel? There are several things to consider when choosing a college route.

6

DECEMBER

"We did it! We have literally completed and submitted all of our college applications! So that accomplishment calls for a celebration!" Jake has an ear-to-ear smile on his face. He's so cute. His smile is my favorite feature, besides his kind heart, of course!

"Right??? Now we wait!" I make a goofy face like I'm freaking out with stress.

I've been struggling with this, but I recently resolved between therapy and writing in my journal, NOT to let it take over my thoughts and ruin my happy times when I'm with Jake, my friends, or family. It's taken me a good month or more to get to this point.

I also finally came clean to Jake about my sincere fears and trepidations regarding Jake getting in, and what if I didn't, or if we both did, or neither did, or I got in and Jake didn't?

I mean, my head was spinning while I was baring my soul to Jake during Thanksgiving break.

Oh, another thing I need to add: remember, Jake was a sweetie in Hawaii and said he had some ideas and plans for us, and he's going to college??

Well, bless his heart, those all went out the window when he had to look into which universities had a good public broadcasting bachelor's and master's program, and that would be UT Austin.

Anyway, the entire discussion went down on Sunday night before we were to return to school after our Thanksgiving Break. We'd played games in the afternoon, had enjoyed many rounds of leftovers, and Jake and his family and my family were all in the family room laughing and talking.

My mind was full of too many thoughts to just sit there, so I excused myself to get some pie from the kitchen. While I was rooting around in the fridge for the pie and whipped cream, I noticed there were quite a few dishes ready to be rinsed and loaded into the dishwasher. I locked into doing just that. I don't know how much time passed, but I was obviously in a thought bubble elsewhere, because I didn't hear someone come into the kitchen until I instantly smelled Jake's cologne. He gave me a hug from behind and nestled his face in my hair.

"Hey, Gracie! What are you doing? I was missing you!" Jake lets me go, and I turn around and face him.

"Oh, hey, Jake, sorry. I came in to get some leftovers, but saw there were some dishes left to be rinsed and loaded in, so I thought I'd help out," I tell him.

"Did you ever get any food? Do you want some more pie?"

"Absolutely. Lots of whipping cream, pretty please." I smile.

I watch as Jake cuts two pieces of pumpkin pie and squirts so much whipped cream on top of both pieces. I grab two forks and two napkins and follow Jake out of the kitchen.

"Porch?" he asks me.

"Yes please!" I respond happily.

The weather was delightful. We eat our pie and put the plates down on the ground far enough away so that we don't drag our feet through the remains. We love sitting out on my porch (yes, we usually are at my house), swinging in the new porch swing Kenneth got us. And this is where we find ourselves again as we eat and chat idly. Jake and I adore it!

We were just enjoying the cooler temps, each other's company, and the solitude of a quiet night, when Jake asked me how my essays for admissions had been coming along.

"Ummmm, yeah, pretty good!" Lie. I hated the essays. I wasn't sure what to write, so I'd been dragging my feet on this.

"Yeah. That's a super sketch response!" He laughs.

"Yep. True that. So what I need to say is that I'm stuck. I'm just not that interesting a person. What life lessons have I experienced? I didn't want to use my dad's passing because I'm hardly the only kid who's lost a parent." I sigh a long sigh.

"Umm, Grace. That's exactly what you need to write about. Your experience is unique and distinct from that of others. I promise you that much," he assures me.

"Really??"

"Really."

"Okay. That helps me a lot. I'll finish them this week. But Jake, there's more. I've a few thoughts that I've been holding onto for too long. I didn't want to burden you. I didn't want to take away from your excitement to go to UT-A. But. Let's be real. I'm not a strong candidate. And I know this. Additionally, I've been seriously considering staying here to earn my associate's degree.

And be with Beth. And at the same time, my heart is shredding thinking of us being apart. We see each other every day. What if this really happens, and what do we do about it?" I ask.

Dang it. Tears start to trickle from my eyes.

"Sweet girl!" Jake stops the swing and faces me straight on. "Gracie! Regardless, we will be together. I can't speak to whether you'll get in, I'll get in, or both, or neither, but I have given the whole matter some serious thought. I've been talking to my dad, actually, and he's been helping me sort through this all: I don't want to break up, no matter what, before college. You're my person. So we met in high school? Doesn't mean we can't keep living life and dating until we want to, you know, make it all more permanent and forever."

Jake takes a breath. I'm sure he noticed that my eyes about bugged out of my head. I was sooooo shocked by his words.

"And," he continues, "no matter what, we'll still be boyfriend and girlfriend. Even if I'm a couple of hours away, or you are. You're my person, Grace. I never want what happened to my parents to happen to us. I want our relationship to be solid. For us to become united on all fronts. And if we're not, I want us to work through it so we can. Sorry Grace. I know that was a lot to share, but I've suspected you've been keeping a brave face for my sake. You don't have to. I feel the same way as you. We will do our best, regardless of whether we are at the same college or not. Okay?"

"I'm your person?"

Jake bursts into laughter.

"That's what you got from all of what I just said to you?"

"No, I mean, yeah, I mean, my emotions are flowing overboard! I've never thought I'd be anyone's person. Let alone yours…." My voice trails off. I can't help it. My heart is going to explode with happiness. This BOY!!!

"Okay." I take a breath. "Okay, Jake. I'm in. I'm all in. No matter what! No matter what happens.

Okay??!! We can do it. I know we can. Because, as you already know, Jake, that you've been my person and you always will be!"

There was a lot of hugging and kissing after all of this. Dang. It was very, very magical.

To say the least. This whole evening would warrant a mirror chat and at least four journal entries.

I can't even put into words how I feel. To be Jake's person is, as I said, insane. Dreamy. Amazing.

There are not enough beautiful words to express, but from that point on, the worry train in my brain has traveled on.

I'm done—no more. Idc what happens, I know where we stand. I know things will work out. No matter what!

7

JANUARY

I DON'T LIKE the month of January. I know, sort of silly, but the overall color scheme outdoors is so brown and gray—blah.

I'm a very sun-out-feel-happy kinda girl. Additionally, this month is going to become the longest ever, as all seniors in the nation await acceptance letters from colleges.

It's also a very wintery month, as is February, in North Texas. Any cold snaps or freezes that occur happen in January and February. So, that makes January extra blah for me.

School is cruising by, and classes are good—lots of homework. The library study sessions are a plus though, 'cause we can see each other *and* get work done.

Plus, I love the library. Books galore! Whenever I need a brain break, I peruse some of my favorite book sections. I love the front covers of books. Oh, and titles.

It's got to be an awesome front cover and title, except for a nonfiction book for school or in general. That's how I choose what to read.

Of course, once I start it and find I don't like it, then I'll stop reading it. And move on to my next choice.

I'm not a "bestseller" reader at all. They usually disappoint. I enjoy picking and choosing fictional books that share a message with the reader. And pull me in right away with the first sentence.

Anyway, I just went on a wild book tangent, ha, ha, but as I was saying, I love the library and, let me add, bookstores!

I once read that you should keep books that bring you joy. My collection of books is just that, as I've been working on collecting them for many years.

Saying all this reminds me of Jake and our first date: we went to the bookstore and got ice cream. And he bought me a book. It was so romantic to me and super sweet.

Now, we go to bookstores often and are at the library three times a week, so books and reading are an integral part of our lives. I love this so much.

We are getting ready to head home now. Another Thursday night came and went.

Also, there is one more day in the school week. Then the weekend! My thoughts fluctuate from "there are five months left until gradua-tion" to "I hope I get into UT Austin," but I'm not fretting—pinky promise.

I just let thoughts flow through my brain and out. I won't dwell on any one thing, which makes my stress level manageable.

Saturday, Brooke, Justin, Jake, and I thought we'd go ice skating. The Houston area features an impressive ice rink located at the base of The Galleria, a popular mall. It's incredible.

We are all pretty decent skaters, so we spend a good hour or so and go with the flow of the music. Jake takes my hand and we skate around and around for a lot of songs. As we are skating, I see that Justin and Brooke are doing the same thing: holding hands.

"I hope they stay together, don't you?" I say to Jake. I point at Brooke and Justin.

"Yeah, me too. They do make a cute couple. But who knows? People can change as they get older, I guess," Jake says.

I smile at him, but I get a tinge of panic in my heart hearing him say THAT.

PEOPLE CAN CHANGE AS THEY GET OLDER? WHAT THE HECK DOES THAT MEAN? US? OR SOMEONE ELSE?

I swallow hard and pretend that what Jake said hasn't just made me completely stressed! In fact, I'm so distracted by this weird comment that I end up tripping and pulling Jake down too, and we both end up in an embarrassing heap in the middle of the rink! It's funny enough, though, that we bust up laughing.

"Are you okay, Jake? I'm soooo clumsy!" I say in a mixed voice of trembling and laughing.

"All good! That was great! I don't even know how we managed to do that!" he chuckles.

Brooke and Justin come to check on us.

"What the heck happened!!" Brooke squeals. "Are you guys okay? It looked really bad from where we were when you went down, Gracie, but hilarious when you grabbed Jake and he flopped on top of you!"

"Yeah, dude, are you guys cool?" Justin asks, laughing.

Jake and I pick ourselves up, all the while laughing, and it's then that I realize my stress is gone because of the goofy fall. I *also* realize that Jake is talking about his parents. Not us. DUH.

We manage to skate around without any issues until the very end, when Brooke and Justin both end up on their butts! Jake and I skate over to reciprocate their kindness and check on them!

"Okay, I think we've reached the end of our good luck," I say with giggly tears coming down my cheeks.

"Laugh it up Gracie!" Brooke tries to sound serious, but she's giggling. Fortunately, we're almost at the end of our skate time, as it's nearly 3:00 pm, when elementary kids get to have free run of the rink on weekends.

"That was SO fun!" Brooke says to us all. We all agree. As we take off our skates and change into our shoes, she asks me if I'm ready.

"Umm, for what?" I say, innocently laughing.

"Gracie! PLEASE!!" She whines.

"Kidding, relax Brooke. I know, I know. We need to shop for dresses and shoes!" I roll my eyes and continue tying my shoes. I immediately start envisioning what this shopping adventure will be like!!

I hope I survive it! Brooke gets very intense when it comes to shopping. She's literally a black belt! She gets laser-focused, and you have to try on so many items! ARGH.

"Gracie? Hello?" Jake laughs as he waves his hand in front of my eyes.

"I'm here. I'm awake. I was just thinking about how shopping with Brooke *could* go today!! I'm a little nervous. I need a dressier dress and dressy sandals. Up to now, I've only gone shopping with her for casual clothes," I say.

Jake laughs again. "I do love your brain. You're a funny girl. I'm sure it will be fine. Just one thought for you to hold onto: don't let her make you get something you know you won't feel comfortable in. What do you think about that idea?"

I give him a little grin. "Excellent advice. I will take that thought with me because you know Brooke. Love her. But she has very strong opinions!"

"Yeah, she does. That's what I'm getting at. Be prepared to say now and to say how you really feel."

We four continue to banter with each other as we walk toward the video game arcade to drop off Jake and Justin.

"Have so much fun, you two! Pray for me!" I say to Jake and Justin as they go into the arcade.

"Would you please chill?" Brooke huffs at me.

"I'm just kidding!" I give Brooke a wry smile.

But I'm not really kidding. Brooke has become a good friend to me, for sure. But the girl has some serious fashion opinions that she won't let go of. Loves to share and wants to make sure that I never digest those opinions! It's a lot sometimes. But in a good way.

"So, which store first?" I ask with added glee in my voice.

"Zara. Then Nordstrom," Brooke says resolutely.

"Ohhhh. I love Zara. And I adore Nordstrom."

"Okay. So here's my plan. We are in search of an LBD: little black dress—and some strappy black sandals with a thick heel," Brooke states matter-of-factly.

"Sounds good to me." Idk what the heck kind of LBD I'll even be able to find today, but I do trust Brooke, and I sincerely hope the strappy sandals she has me try on aren't too high! I wouldn't want to trip and fall face-first during the graduation ceremony.

"Okay, let's do this!" Brooke says, as I follow her, like a little puppy follows its owner.

Brooke starts slapping racks and piling items over her arm. I continue to follow her.

"I have about ten different types of LBDs I want you to try." Brooke is staring me right in the eyes. "Your goal is to try on every single one. No matter what. We need to rule out what works and doesn't work with your figure and height."

I nod in agreement and follow her to the dressing rooms.

I hope I survive this! I kid, but let's be real: Ten dresses are a lot to try on, and this is just the first store.

But, to be fair, I trust Brooke completely. Here I go!!

I try on EVERY SINGLE DRESS, one at a time. Brooke analyzes every. Single. One.

Too tight. Too long. Too ruffly. Too plain. Hate the side zipper and on and on.

But! Rest assured, I did find one. Number seven is the winner, winner, chicken dinner!

THANK THE HEAVENS ABOVE!! I vetoed the too-short dresses. Number seven is knee-length. Fitted with a beautiful square neckline (I didn't know that was a thing, but it is).

And there are V-neck, round, sweetheart, etc, etc., all sorts of necklines they're called. And, I will admit, it is super flattering on my neck and face.

It zips in the back and has stretch, so I can breathe while walking. That's a huge plus for me. Some of them had no give whatsoever— they were awful! Oh!

And it was only $145 out the door with tax—that's a great price. I have been saving my money for a long time, so I have plenty to pay for the dress.

"Well done, Gracie. I have to say that I am impressed with you. I threw a lot of dresses at you, and you came out with a terrific LBD." Brooke smiles her gorgeous smile at me, her white teeth sparkling and her pink lips perfectly shaped with just the right amount of lipstick.

Note to self: ask Brooke what she wears on her lips! I keep forgetting to ask her.

Dress, paid for, and wrapped in a clothing protector, we make our way to Nordstrom for shoes. I sent a quick text to Jake.

Grace <hey found a dress>

Jake <awesome how painful was it Ha ha>

Grace <I survived lol, but seriously, Brooke is really good at this stuff, although I did ask her why we were shopping so early for graduation, to which she told me that all the good dresses would be scooped up and purchased if we didn't get this done now>

Jake < are you girls off to try on shoes?>

Grace <yep wish me luck lol>

Jake <:P>

I am following Brooke into the women's show department while texting Jake, trying to keep up with her very long and tan legs; she's about two full inches taller than I am.

"Okay, here's my vision: black, straps, chunky heel, platforms, or a wedge heel. So, let's do it the same way we did to find your dress. Cool?"

"Cool. And Brooke, thanks. I truly appreciate you helping me." I smile at her.

"It is my pleasure. Be happy you know me." She grins, but she means it.

We circle the shoe area like buzzards scanning the ground for food. Brooke grabs a shoe here and there as we are on circle two.

We find a comfy couch to sit down on, and Giorgio (Brooke's regular shoe salesperson) heads our way.

"Giorgio, this is my friend, Grace. We need dressy, strappy black sandals to go with this dress."

Brooke grabs my covered dress and reveals it to Giorgio.

"Ah, perfetto, so beautiful!" Giorgio says in his very thick Italian-laced accent.

"Right? We tried on so many, but this one looks amaze on her," Brooke tells Giorgio, and then they go into a full shoe convo, which I'm simply overhearing.

Then, Giorgio takes the sample shoes with him to the back room.

"He's the best. I've come to him ever since I moved here," Brooke tells me.

"Cool," I say, 'cause idk what it's like to have my own shoe sales-person at a major department store!

Less than ten minutes pass, and Giorgio emerges with ten boxes of shoes! Five under each arm!

Sheesh! Here we go again! Lol.

I have to try on each pair of shoes while holding my dress up. Fortunately for my sake, by the fifth sandal, Brooke says, "This is the one!"

I am so happy and relieved as Giorgio packs it up, and I head toward the register to pay—$100 total for the shoes.

"I know both the dress and shoes cost a good amount of money, but you want quality and style over any trendy items for this event. High school graduation only happens once unless you're a vampire!" Brooke laughs and watches as Giorgio hands me my shoes.

Brooke is holding my dress until I get my shoe bag situated in my hands. She gives me my dress, and we walk out of Nordstrom and find the down escalator.

"I'm ready to eat! I'm so hungry!" Brooke dramatically whines to me.

"Me too! Shopping can *really* work up an appetite!" I laugh as we descend to meet up with the boys.

"Let's just go through a drive-through and eat at the park by my house, how about you guys?" I suggest we walk to Jake's Rubicon. Justin parked his Land Cruiser next to Jake.

"Yeah, that sounds chill," Justin says. "I just need food!"

"Ditto," Jake chimes in.

"Yeah, we're starving too!" Brooke says as she grabs Justin's hand and moves in close to him.

They really are a sweet couple. Good thing Justin hung in there all year with the high hopes of going out with Brooke, which didn't happen until after Brooke woke up from her coma, but at least it DID happen! Justin had to be the most patient person EVER because WHEN Brooke woke up, he was both happy and flustered at the same time when she asked to see him immediately! Watching Justin kiss Brooke for the first time was a magical moment. Jake and I were so happy for them both! FINALLY!

We all four walk to the old picnic table that's still in good shape at our little park. Jake and I sit on one side of the table, and Brooke and Justin take the other side. Everyone is silent for like ten minutes as we consume our food like ravenous wolves.

Brooke and Justin finish up first and walk toward the swings. I watch them swing for a bit while Jake and I finish our food.

"I'm so glad Brooke gave Justin a chance," I muse.

"For real. Oh hey! I won you a little prize. I was so hungry I completely forgot! Waiting for you girls to shop really amped up our appetites!" Jake laughs as he says this to me.

"Try being the shopper!! I had to work *so hard* to find the perfect outfit! Holy!!" We both laugh as Jake pulls out the cutest teeny white fluffy sheep with little purple ears and hooves.

The four of us hang out for almost another hour together, taking turns swinging on the two swings and teeter-tottering.

"Hey, Brooke and Justin, y'all ready to go back? I'm so exhausted!" Jake yells to them.

"Me too!" I chime in.

"Yeah, we're coming," Brookes says. We clean up our trash, and each boy grabs their significant other by the hand, and we walk back to my house.

"Bye, guys. I had such a great day with y'all!" I say to both Brooke and Justin.

"Us too," Brooke says.

"Ditto," says Justin as he shuts his car door and starts up Brooke's new blue Mustang her parents bought her last summer after her accident. Justin doesn't mind driving it, but Brooke won't drive in his Honda, ha ha, yeah, there's that!

Jake and I wave goodbye to them and sit on my steps for a few minutes. It's nearly 9 pm and I'm so tired I can barely keep awake!

"Well, another great day with you and our cute friends! Thanks for the ice skating. It was really fun. We need to do that again. And thank you for being a good sport, hanging out with Justin at the arcade. I know that's not really your vibe, so I appreciate it," I say.

"To be honest, it was super fun. I found a few games I could play pretty well for a newbie. And, of course, it's never a problem to support you, because you do the same for me. I'm just glad you found a great outfit, too. Check that off your list!" he smiles.

"For real." I lean in as does Jake, and we share a lingering, soft kiss.

"Night, Gracie-Lou," he says softly.

"Night," I whisper.

SIGHHHHHHHH I adore that beautiful boy!

8

___

FEBRUARY

"Congratulations, Jake!!" Mom kisses his cheek. I'm loitering near him. He's beaming with pride at his accomplishment.

We're all gathered in the family room. It's Sunday—family game day and hang-out day.

Even Zac and Sarah are in town for the weekend, so it's been a party since Friday night!

We went out to dinner. We're going to the movies and shopping on Saturday, and then we'll chill together today. College acceptance letters are arriving.

I am so excited for Jake. He deserves the very best. He just got his yesterday.

I was accepted into our community college last week; now I am just waiting for the University of Texas at Austin.

I'm hoping that I'm next to get my acceptance letter sooner rather than later—trying to KEEP CALM. TRYING is the keyword.

After a few hours of games, the dinner prep begins. The adults are handling it all today.

Fine with me!! When everything is prepped and served, we settle down at the table.

We decided to gather for an impromptu Sunday dinner after church and games—even Jake's parents are here (even his mom!).

Everyone is sitting by their significant other, or bestie, in Meg and Beth's case.

I am smiling as I look around the table (we have two leaves we can put in to seat up to fourteen people!). My heart is full. These are ALL my people—minus my beautiful dad, of course.

I continue to chew and muse over this group. I allow myself to move my eyes to Dad's wall.

My eyes linger on some of my favorite pictures: Dad with the three of us kids at the beach when we visited his dad's favorite aunt. There have been yearly family photos since Mom and Dad were married, and each year thereafter until he passed away. I pause on one of my favorite photos of my dad and me. He had just learned to braid my hair, and we posed to show the finished product. Such a simple picture that brings back so many feelings of love, it almost hurts. I continue to stare at the wall, letting the memories wash over me for a long while.

I feel warmth in my chest. Tears try to gather, but I grab a napkin and wipe my eyes quickly, averting my face.

When do the tears stop? Maybe never? Tears always help me love my dad, though, and remind me of him and his goodness and love for all of us.

I take more bites and focus on the conversations going on around me. I catch snippets here and there.

Looking up, I see my mom looking across the table at me. She sends me an air kiss. I grin and place my hand on my heart. She must have seen me get teary-eyed as I was looking at Dad's wall.

I often wonder how Mom feels these days. She's found a great second husband. But, does she still cry? Of course, she does. There will always be reminders of Dad. And, I know she does. I hear her crying here and there, but none of us is as teary as we once were. Thankfully.

But, there will always be a smell, a sight, a thought, or an item that will forever remind me of my dad. The same goes for Mom, Zac, and Beth. How could we ever forget him? This whole house reminds us of Dad. I mean, Mom has changed some things, made the Dad Wall, and stuff like that.

I'm proud of my mom for still being in this house. I know it was super hard for the first year. Like almost unbearably hard, but Mom did it for us three kids. We love this lovely yellow house and love how safe and secure it is here.

I'm pulled from my reverie by dessert. Beth and Meg whipped up a fabulous dessert: chocolate mousse using box instant chocolate pudding and a container of Cool Whip. It was seriously so delicious! The day ended with laughter and good conversation. Around 8:00 pm, everyone started cleaning up and packing up to head home.

"Bye, Jake! Bye Meg! Bye, Mr. and Mrs. Hansen! Great to have you all over," I call out to Jake and his family, after Jake gives me a delightful kiss on my lips and a hug in the doorway.

I close the door with a smile and a warm feeling that goes from my head to my toes! I stop by the kitchen and help with the last of the cleanup, then we all hug and kiss Zac and Sarah as they leave to stay over at Sarah's house before heading back early tomorrow morning.

Soon, I crawl into my bed—one of my cherished spots in my house—and my mind takes me to the letter-that-hasn't-come-yet and I wonder if that means something or if I am reading too much into the tardiness of the letter? Either way, it sucks.

Maybe it will come this week? Fingers crossed and all that stuff to bring me good luck!!

I put in my AirPods and let myself relax, nodding off to sleep.

BUT ANOTHER WEEK PASSES, AND NO LETTER FOR ME.

Okay, I am NOT going to freak out, but I'm freaking out. I'm trying to hide it, but danggggg, what if? NOPE. Not going there.

And then the next Monday, the letter arrives.

Dear Grace Miller,

We regret to inform you that you were not accepted to attend UT of A this fall. Please apply again next semester.

Thank you for applying. We wish you good luck!
Signed,
Dean Hutchinson

I freeze. I'm standing in the kitchen. Frozen like an ice cube in a glass.

Jake had just dropped Beth and me off. It's a Tuesday—volunteering day. Beth is eating graham crackers and milk at the table.

She hasn't noticed that I haven't moved an inch for like five minutes. Suddenly, she's by my side. "Gracie? What's wrong? Gracie?!"

I turn to Beth. I hand her the letter.

"Read it!" Just like Jane tells Elizabeth to read the letter from Charles Bingley's pernicious sister in *Pride and Prejudice.*

This letter feels pernicious. It feels like a dagger to my heart. A pinprick that just popped my balloon of good future plans.

"Oh, Gracie, I am so sorry. Boy, that is ONE SHORT letter for all the crap you guys had to do to apply. Sheesh. Wait. Does Jake know? Mom or Kenneth?" Beth asks.

I shake my head, indicating a no, and feel a wave of fear and trepidation wash over me. I almost lose my balance.

"Okay, let's go see Mom. She's just come home and is lying on the couch in her office for a bit. Kenneth is at the grocery store, getting the goods for our monthly pizza night," Beth is telling me, but nothing is registering.

"I think the homemade pizza will be a perfect comfort food for tonight since you got this stupid letter," Beth adds, since I've said nothing at all. Beth puts her arm in mine and guides me into Mom's office.

She has my letter still clutched in her hands.

"MOMMMM," Beth yells to Mom. I'm not registering much. I just let Beth continue to guide me.

"What's going on? Gracie?" Mom sounds concerned.

Beth hands our mom the letter. She reads it. A sad expression appears on her face.

"Can you help her sit in her favorite chair, please, Beth?" Mom asks. Beth does so.

"Oh dear. Jake is in. Grace is not. Oh. Dear." Mom looks from Beth to me as she's putting two and two together.

"Grace? Grace?!" Mom keeps saying my name to get me to respond. I finally snap out of my daze.

"It happened. Just what I DID NOT want to happen, HAPPENED!" I say to my mom. "Now what?"

"Soooo, I guess you haven't told Jake yet?" Mom grimaces as she asks this question because she already knows the answer.

"No," I say in a teeny voice.

"No, I guess not, since you just got the letter today. Okay, so now, you're asking me, what do you do? Now, you go with your other plan: go to the community college and get your associate's degree there," she replies logically.

I'm glad Mom can be reasonable, because I feel absolutely miserable. "And have a stupid long-distance relationship with Jake since he'll be two hours away from me, and then he'll meet someone in Austin and realize that I am NOT his person and that this for me was all a dream!"

Mom sighs. "Yep, unfortunately, that is something that COULD happen, but I do trust Jake. I believe you two are a great match. And, yes, being apart definitely makes a relationship much more challenging. But, many people have done this before, so I know it is possible, it's just not easy, I guess is what I'd say."

I look at Mom and nod.

"Sweetie, just sit here for a bit, okay? Or would you rather go lie on your bed for a bit to digest all of this?" Mom asks kindly.

"Yeah, thanks, guys," I mumble. "Sorry to be a Debbie Downer. I'll see you at dinnertime. CRAP. I need to text everyone to say I won't be able to go and volunteer today. I can't even think straight!"

"Beth," Mom turns to face her. "Do you have time to help Kenneth and me with dinner prep when he gets back from the store?"

"Sure, Mom. Grace, go chill. Pop in your AirPods and drown out the noise of your brain for a bit." Beth pats my shoulder, and she and Mom walk out of Mom's studio.

I drag myself up onto my feet and slowly walk out of the office. I quietly shut the door behind me. I continue my slow walk up the stairs. Push my bedroom door open and fling myself onto my bed.

Facedown. And then the waterworks begin. I sob like I'm a kid whose ice cream scoops fell off her cone onto the dirty sidewalk. I cry and cry.

How can so much good and happiness be flowing in and around me, and then THIS HAPPENS???

I know I told myself it would be just fine if this happened, but, obviously, I'm a crappy liar to myself and others!

THIS news is not what I wanted for myself at all! Dang it. Crapppity crap. I am soooooooooo upset.

I flip myself over. I grab my phone and text the group.

Grace <guys-feeling really sick-can't come today>

Brooke <okay-sorry, Gracie, feel better>

Justin <bummer>

Jake <Gracie? I'll text you separately>

Crappity crap. Jake will see right through my lie. What can I even say?

PING.

It's Jake.

Jake <what's up? I didn't know you didn't feel good today>

Grace <yeah, no big deal, just started after you dropped us off, just gonna rest>

Jake < Okay, I can swing by after the volunteer shift>

Grace <no, no, not tonight. I'll just see you in the a.m>

Jake <okay, sure, feel better>

If I know Jake well, and I do, he will be over to my house immediately after his volunteering shift.

I will have to tell him sooner rather than later, meaning tonight or tomorrow at the latest, so might as well rip off the bandage tonight and not wait.

I pop in my AirPods and drown my sorrows in my music.

I must have fallen asleep for a bit because, at some point, I feel someone shaking my shoulder.

"Grace? Jake's downstairs. Time to wake up. I saved your dinner in the fridge, too, whenever you're hungry," Mom says.

"Jake is here? I look terrible. Can you tell him to give me five minutes, please, Mom?"

"Of course, sweetie." Mom gives me a reassuring smile as she leaves my room. She closes my door behind her.

I look crazy.

I brush my hair and throw it up into a scrunchie. I check my face, brush my teeth, and smooth my dress.

Here I go! I'm not looking forward to this, but there's no choice.

"WISH ME LUCK MIRROR!" I say it with intense emotion, but in a quiet, raspy voice.

I can hear Jake talking with Kenneth and my mom as I slowly descend the staircase.

Boy, I wish I were going anywhere right now instead of having to go downstairs to tell my boyfriend that I didn't get into a college that I should have technically gotten accepted to! I have good grades! I'm smart! What the actual heck is happening?? I wish I could ask someone, WHYYYYYY I didn't get accepted?

They're in our family room.

Jake stands immediately as I enter the family room. Kenneth and Mom excuse themselves.

Mom gives my arm a little squeeze as she passes me by.

"Hey Gracie, you okay?" Jake eyes me up and down.

"Yeah, yeah, I'm better now. I dozed off for a bit. Just woke up."

"Okay, good. I was worried about you."

"Nah, no need to worry. How was the shift? I hated to bail." I tried to sound nonchalant.

I truly hated to bail, but I couldn't go when I was literally having an emotional breakdown!

"Everyone missed you. The other volunteers all said to tell you hi." Jake grins.

"Oh, that's so sweet! I missed them, too." I smile back at him.

His brow furrows with worry. "You sure you're okay? You seem abnormally mellow."

"Um, ha, yeah, you noticed that? Well, I got a letter from UT of A, and, ummm…." Tears spring to my eyes, and I pull the letter from my pocket and thrust it at Jake.

"Here. Read it," I say for the second time today.

Jake takes the letter. Unfolds it and starts to read it.

He looks up at me, drops my letter onto the couch, and walks over to me, enfolding me into a hug.

Of course, I cry. Again. Jake lets me cry for a bit.

Then, needing a Kleenex, I pull away and grab one from the box on the coffee table.

"Grace, I'm sorry. I just can't believe you didn't get in. Like, what?" He shakes his head.

I dab my nose. "Yeah, Super sucks."

"Yeah, that's an understatement."

"Yeah."

We sit in silence for a bit. I can hear the *tick-tock* of the grandfather clock in the front entry area.

It's all I can listen to. Finally, I decided to break the silence.

"So, yeah, now I'll stay here for fall and you'll go away to Austin." My words come out very choppy. Almost staccato.

"Um, I guess so. Not the way I envisioned our fall semester starting…." Jake's voice trails off. He takes a deep breath and blows it out.

"Nope." I do the same. Innnnn. Outtttt.

We sit in silence again. I pick at my fingernail.

Jake is tapping his foot. I don't think we've had this type of feeling occur between us yet.

I am feeling weird and awkward. So, I start talking about nothing significant, trying to stop feeling uncomfortable.

"Uh, so the weather has been really nice this week, right? Maybe we can go for a nice long walk tomorrow after school? You know? Get some fresh air and all. Ha- ha. Never enough of that fresh air for us high schoolers in school all day, ha-ha," I say.

And yes, I continue talking. "Hey, ummm, you gotta go, Jake, it's getting late, school tomorrow, and all. Thanks for stopping by. And hey, I'll be just fine. I just need to cry a few million times more, and I'll feel some resolution! No big deal. Really." I give Jake the best smile I can conjure up, given how un-smiley I really feel.

"Yeah, you're a terrible liar, ha-ha, nice try. But yeah, I do need to go. But Grace," he tenderly places his hand on my jaw and turns my head towards him, "I know this is not our ideal situation, but I do think we can make it work. Not gonna be easy, but it is worth it to me if it's worth it to you!"

"Jake! Of course it's worth it! Why do you think I've been crying? Because I want to BE WITH you, at UT of A, and not separated from you, so yeah, it's not gonna be easy one bit, but it will be so worth us staying together and connected, although we'll be far away physically," I insist.

Jake leans in and kisses me. I kiss him back. He pulls back and pushes himself up and off the couch to go towards the front door.

"Hey, let me tell Brooke and Justin, will ya? I don't want to say anything as of yet until I feel better emotionally," I say.

He gives me a sad smile. "Of course, Gracie, of course. Night. See you in the morning."

"See you tomorrow, and thanks for coming over. It was very sweet of you." I follow him to the front door.

I stand in the doorway watching as he jumps into his Rubicon and pulls out. He waves. I wave back.

SIGHHHHHHHHHHHHHHHHHHHHHHHHHHHHHHHHHHHHHH-HHH. Well, not as bad as I was expecting, but still a rather depressing interaction.

Blast. Dang, Crap. I hope to feel less emotional in a few weeks. I HOPE.

9

MARCH

Spring break is almost here. I'm so stoked.

The last one as a high schooler.

My family and I've decided to do a stay-cation—a week of activities you've never done or would like to do, in your actual city.

Cool with me. I'd rather sit and read my books, to be honest, so I suggest we work that into the week we're off.

How am I feeling about everything? Better.

Well, still can't believe I didn't get in, and yeah, I'm sure I could have or should have applied to a few other places, but it's sort of a twisted blessing, as I call it.

I'll be here with Beth for the two years it should take for me to get my associate's degree.

Not like she's asking me, too—it just worked out this way.

Jake and I have talked about what it means. What if he comes one weekend? I go next, etc. We shall see. That may or may not be possible every weekend. We can always FaceTime.

And es obvio (Spanish for obviously), we will text nonstop. My lovely brain likes to add its own what-ifs, and these what-ifs are like this: what if Jake meets someone else? What if Jake is too busy to FaceTime or visit, etc.? There were very fun what-ifs.

However, my therapist suggested that I write down both the ugly what-ifs and the good what-ifs.

My good ones are these: what if we stay solid as a couple, keep our heads down, work hard each week, and meet up each weekend? We can study together. We can have day-dates and so forth.

So, I'm compiling a list and adding to it as thoughts arise. It's actually been truly helpful. It's helping me work through my emotions with the not-so-fun what-ifs—preparing myself mentally for those possible scenarios that could come to fruition!

I see my therapist regularly. I thought I didn't need to go back, but I realize it is a necessity for me and my emotional health.

Now, I am calmer. I can handle these rough, up-and-down emotional rollercoaster rides I continue to be on. I can work through my emotional struggles wayyyyy better.

How's Jake? He's been really happy about being accepted into UT Austin, but not so glad that I didn't get in.

And, unfortunately, he has been caught up in his mother's emotional instability and fickleness. The bad news is that his mother is leaving. This time for good. She just isn't the type to be a mother or stay married, apparently, which has put a big emotional strain on both Jake and Meg.

We see them a lot more for meals again, just as we did last time their mom was away.

I don't mind, though. I actually feel that these past months have really helped us to learn how to support each other with our personal issues, especially with Jake's mom leaving, which has been terrible and so sad. It's broken my heart for him, especially because I know he and Meg way better now, and though Jake says he can handle it, I don't see how anyone can just "handle that." A parent—especially a mother—is important in a child's life—I mean, duh—but even when you're older, these things affect you.

Okay, and yeah, not on the same level, but my rejection letter has thrown me off kilter, and my future plans, I mean, not on the same level whatsoever as Jake and Meg, but for little ol' me, it's been sucky.

I'm hoping Jake will share more with me, and I hope I can be a good support to him. I'm trying. I really am. This is new territory for me. I know how to support my family and friends, but Jake's mom leaving is a whole new level.

All things considered, it's been a rough couple of weeks, so we decided that this Saturday, we need to distract ourselves with a super fun activity, and that activity is bowling!

"Finally! Saturday! Hallelujah! And we're going bowling!" I say to my stuffie, my bed, my mirror, all the inanimate objects around me! But I'm happy today because I hope bowling can help Jake, Meg, and their dad feel a bit of happiness and distract them from their sadness.

"Whose turn is it now?" I'm looking at the blasted game board, but can't see my name. *Oh! There it is. Patience, Gracie—sheesh, girl—apparently, once I bowl, it takes a minute or two to pop up.*

"Ha, never mind. It's me! My second time to bowl. Man, I haven't played this for a hot minute. I almost forgot what I'm doing!" I say, turning to my team and wondering if anyone is listening.

Meg, Jake, Beth, and I are on one team. The adults are all on the other team: Mom, Kenneth, and Jake's dad, Samuel.

I take my turn. I nearly had another gutter ball, but thankfully, I hit the last three pins on my second roll.

I turn to go and sit by Jake. I'm trying to read his facial expression. To me, he looks indifferent.

"Hey, you, how are you holding up?" I ask.

Jake sighs. "I'm okay. I just don't get my mom. I wish I could understand what her deal is or why she keeps doing this, ya know? And my poor dad. Dang it."

I grab his hand and squeeze it. I am looking straight into his gorgeous blue eyes. "I am truly sorry. Not something any of us need right now, nor is it something we planned on happening, especially with graduation just two months away. How's Meg holding up?" I turn to see that she's up to bowl. She's laughing at something Beth said.

I turn 'round to hear Jake answer my question.

"She's doing better than I am, that's for sure. Maybe 'cause I'm older? I don't know, or maybe she keeps her feelings to herself, which, in that case, is not a good thing. How would you feel about asking Beth to do a little recon and see how Meg is *really* doing?" he asks. "She's always pretty upbeat with me and my dad."

"Sure, I'll ask," I say. "She is pretty much always upbeat. I don't even think I've seen her down or grumpy, well, ever!"

Jake nods in agreement. Then, he's up to bowl. He gets a strike. He's freaking good at bowling, who knew??!!

"Beth, you're up!" he calls to his sister.

She grabs her bowling ball and takes her two turns. Beth knocks down seven pins, then gets the other three on her next turn! She's great at everything she does. For real.

Then it's me again. I get a gutter bowl on my first attempt and hit seven on my second.

I try to resume the convo with Jake before it's his turn again. "So, um, when did your mom leave, like officially?"

"Yesterday. She flew back to California to try to *find herself* or something like that," he replies bitterly. "At this point, I'm just over it all and don't want to text or talk with her for a while. I can't handle her emotional ups and downs. I thought for sure this past year she'd stick around for good. Then, she got antsy in January and hasn't been in a good emotional state since then."

"Ugh, I am so sorry, I didn't realize it had been that long. I'm sorry, Jake. What can I do to help you guys?" I ask.

"This type of thing helps a lot." He gestures to the bowling alley. "Other than distracting ourselves, Meg and I do our schoolwork, and Dad just works hard. Coming over for dinners when he's working late has been good for both Meg and me. I'm sorry I didn't tell you that sooner. Oh! I'm up!"

I watch as he rises and gets his ball. He's almost six feet now. I'm a whopping 5'8", but hey, we're a good match height-wise, at least.

Jake gets a spare.

"Great job! Well, Jake and Meg are creaming us, Beth! We need to step it up." I laughingly say to my sister.

"Speak for yourself, sis. I'm ahead of you!" She laughs right at me.

"Crud, *I* need to step it up!" I smile, and we continue playing for the next hour.

Then, we all pile into the cars and drive to our favorite Tex-Mex restaurant, Mi Cocina. Jake and I have eaten here quite a bit together. I love their enchiladas, their salsa, and chips! Samuel, Jake's dad, orders us a few appetizers to eat before we each order whatever we want to eat for dinner.

Once we've eaten and talked for a while, it's time to call it a night. Jake drove us all, so he dropped Beth and me off.

Meg and her dad, Samuel, pop into my house to say hello to my mom and Kenneth, and Meg, to get an ice cream sandwich for the road, leaving Jake and me alone for a bit.

"Jake, thanks for talking to me about your mom. I know it's not a great subject, but I appreciate you confiding in me," I say.

He shrugs. "I am trying to communicate better, since I did so poorly that one time and broke your heart."

My face reddens with embarrassment.

"Yeah, that was not my favorite, but look at us now? I know from watching my parents that they had to really work on their communication together. My dad kept everything inside, then would periodically tell my mom that he wasn't doing well mentally, and she'd be totally shocked and amazed," I explained, thinking back.

Then, I continued. "They ended up going to my mom's therapist together to work on that. I know it took a good year or two to get better at it. Seeing them do that has made it a priority for me, and well, now with you, it's becoming an even bigger priority."

"I sure wish my mom and dad would have done something like that, but I have an inkling that my mom has always been this way—a free spirit —and that once we were old enough, she knew. I could handle taking care of Meg. Not cool, but I guess I can see her reasoning." Jake grimaced.

We both turn to see Meg come out of the front door with two ice cream sandwiches. I lean over, hug Jake, and kiss his cheek.

"Have a good rest of your night. I'll text you when I'm ready to go to sleep."

"Gracie, thanks." He gives his 100-watt smile, and my wee little heart melts with happiness.

I jump down from the passenger side of his Rubicon and walk to my door. I turn around and wave to them both.

I am a lucky girl. I really am. Jake is such a great human. Sigh. I haven't said the L word as of yet, but it's been on the tip of my tongue quite a bit.

I want to wait until we're in college to see how things go before I tell Jake I love him.

Oh! I need to talk with Beth about Meg. I can't forget!

I close the door behind me and meander up the stairs toward my room, but first, I stop at Beth's room.

"Hey, chica!" I stand in her doorway.

"Gracie, what's up?" Beth is sitting up on her bed, flipping through a magazine.

"Got a few minutes to talk?" I enter her room and sit on the little green couch in the corner.

"Shoot. What do you want to talk about?" She eyes me slightly suspiciously.

"Ha, relax, it's just about Meg. You obviously know their mom left yesterday."

"Yeah, she told me. But she never says anything about her mom or how she feels about their crazy situation. I've tried to talk to her." She blows out a frustrated breath.

"That's just what I wanted to know so that I can tell Jake. He's on point then, because he's pretty sure she's just been pushing all her feelings deep, deep down inside of her. Blast." I give Beth a smirk.

"He'd be right in assuming all of that. So, since I've tried quite a few times and totally failed to get any info, I'm just letting it go now. I don't want to push her too much, ya know?" she says.

"Yeah, I agree with you. Okay, well, I appreciate your input. I'll let Jake know because, and you won't be shocked at this, Meg doesn't say anything to Jake or his dad either." I rise to leave Beth's room.

"Well, I think having Jake know will get the ball rolling to help Meg, maybe?" Beth gives me a sweet smile.

"True that. Do you think it would be weird to share my therapist's info with Jake for Meg?" I make a wry facial expression.

"Nah, I think that's a good idea. I'm afraid Meg will just burst one day, and that will not be pretty!" Beth nods her head.

"And, Beth? One more thing before I leave, I feel you've done super well in your classes. You've a good rapport with your teachers, and I also think that over the past few months, you've been more upfront and honest with Mom and me. Am I correct in assuming all of this?" I give her a sisterly smile.

"You'd be correct to assume all of this. Interestingly, you mentioned this about Meg tonight. Jake is a good big brother. I've been a bit worried about her. So tell him from me that he's an awesome brother who cares about her." Beth gets up from her bed and turns to walk into the Jack and Jill bathroom she used to share with Zac.

Ahhhh, the Jack and Jill bathroom reminds me of how much I miss Zac.

"I sure miss Zac!" I blurt out to Beth. "Looking at the Jack and Jill bathroom makes me sad to know he's gone, well, I guess forever, since he and Sarah are engaged. Boo. I mean, I'm happy for them, but I miss him! Thank goodness we text a lot. Do you guys text much?"

Zac and I are much closer, but Beth and Zac still have a solid relationship.

"Oh my gosh! I think happy thoughts of Zac every time I use the bathroom! I totally miss him so much, too! And yeah, we text sporadically, so that's super helpful." Beth agreed.

"Ahh, I am so glad you guys text and keep up! I love that for you. Well, I need to head to bed. Love ya, Beth. Sleep well. We had a good day today, didn't we?" I say.

"Love you too, Gracie. We surely did. See you in the morning." She goes back to what she'd been doing before.

I grab the doorknob and close the door as I amble down to my room to get ready for bed.

1 0

APRIL

I'm STANDING by Jake's car—waiting for him to come out and take me home. Beth and Meg have a study group of sorts after school today. I close my eyes—still waiting—and let the sun's rays warm my face.

School let out like ten minutes ago? Where the heck is Jake? He doesn't usually take thissss longgggg . . .

I continue waiting. I open my eyes and am about to text Jake when he's suddenly in front of me, holding the most delicious bunch of sunflowers! They're so large and fully in bloom.

"What in the world?" I say to Jake.

"Gracie, will you go to prom with me, please?" Jake surprises me completely with these words.

"Ohhhh that's so sweet! But you didn't need to go to any trouble! You could have asked me at any time! But, the answer is OF COURSE!" I take the flowers, immediately inhale their fragrance, and give him the biggest hug.

"Excellent! I figure we can go with Brooke and Justin, grab dinner, then head to the dance?" He tells me as he looks at his watch. "Prom is in two weeks, so is that enough time to find a dress?" Jake's facial expression resembles an anime character—his smile is so big and his eyes pleading.

"Absolutely! I've got my shopping stylist, remember? Brooke and I will go look ASAP for dresses." I make a mental note to text her on my way home.

"Phew, thank goodness. I was a little stressed about the time frame, just cause I knew Brooke would need time to find a dress—you, I'm not worried about ha-ha."

"Oh, true that. K. Let's go, and I'll text Brooke right now. Please tell me Justin already asked her?" I say pleadingly.

"Yes! Justin told me he asked Brooke last week. She didn't tell you?" Jake questions.

"Not yet, she went out of town this weekend. Family thingy somewhere." I respond to him.

"Oh, okay, got ya."

We're almost home, and I've already texted Brooke. Waiting for her to pop up.

Knowing her, I bet she's already found a dress. Ugh! It's okay, it will work out! Brooke is the best at shopping, so I'm golden!

Brooke <tell Jake he's so dead! He should have asked you a week ago! BUT it's fine! I actually found this pretty decent online dress company. I bought five dresses and found one that works. Sending back the discards, ha ha. I found a few for you to look at. Hold up. I'll send the pics>

Seven pics came through immediately. Gotta love technology! I scroll through the pics Brooke sent me and see a pale pink dress, long, with a square neck and thick straps. I'm sitting at the kitchen table eating my favorite snack: graham crackers and milk, while I scroll.

Ohhh, I adore this one. Wow. It's so pretty. I'll let Brooke know I love this one and maybe pick two others so she feels like I really took time to look at them!

There's a light blue one I also like. It has a simple scoop neckline and puffed sleeves—I do like it a lot, just not as much as the pale pink dress, and then there's a sea-foam dress. Sweetheart neckline. I like that the least, but it could work.

I sent those three pics back to Brooke. Her rule is YOU MUST TRY ON ANYTHING when shopping. MUST. Unless it's something you've purchased before and are getting in a different color, or a brand you wear a lot and are familiar with their sizing.

Brooke <excellent choices. The pricing is decent too. Each of your dresses range from $115-$135, so if you're able to buy all three in a few different sizes, we can send back the ones that don't work. I'll send you the links for them.>

Gracie <awesome thanks so much! I knew you'd already have a plan in mind!>

Brooke <always <3 >

BY THE END OF TWO WEEKS, I'M READY. DRESSES ACQUIRED. SHOES, too. I did end up getting the pale pink dress (luckily, it fit beautifully) and I found a strappy kitten heel cream shoe to go with it. Brooke got the light blue dress with the sweetheart neckline and puffed sleeves— Brooke looks amazing in everything she puts on. I kid you not!

She's at my house. Her intention is to do my hair AND my makeup for me! FINE BY ME! The guys will be by before 6:00pm, so we have almost four hours to get ready. A little too long for me to primp. But, I take the time to shower, wash my hair and paint my toes and finger nails. Not paying for a mani-pedi—sorry.

Brooke is perfectly manicured, as always, but that's her vibe. Dinner will be at Rocky's Steakhouse and Seafood, a great restaurant located in our downtown square. I'm so excited because I love all of their food. We don't go there more than once a year; it's very gourmet and delish, but spendy. Then we'll make a cameo at the dance, take our obligatory pics, and stay for a bit. Sometimes the dances are pretty lame; we shall see if they can pull it off and make it better for our Senior Prom—fingers crossed!

I can't believe I'm going to PROM! It's one dance I never ever thought I'd attend—I mean, you need to have a really good friend who's a guy to take you, or go with a group of girls, or have a boyfriend. That last category I was never supposed to be in, but here I am! I am super excited! It's a memory I was surely hoping to make—but it was looking very bleak for two years, until Jake Hansen moved here! Now, I can honestly say that all of my dreams have come true!

These thoughts course through my mind as I strap on my other shoe. I stand up and smooth out my dress, and take another look at myself. "Brooke, you're magical! I've never had my hair look this good! And my makeup! So you want to move in and just take care of my clothes, hair and makeup daily? Like for real!"

"You're very welcome. You do have wonderful hair and a great complexion. So that helps." Brooke gives me a smirk as she finishes applying her lipstick. How does she look? AMAZING! Good grief. I feel like a shriveled weed next to her blossomed beautiness! My phone pings.

Jake <on our way! You girls ready?>

Gracie <yep!>

Jake <cool see you in five>

Gracie < <3 >

You know how you watch shows where the girl walks down the stairs looking amazing, and her handsome beau waits for her at the bottom? Well, I'm such a dork, but I have definitely dreamed of this moment many, many times before, and here it was HAPPENING TO ME! Kenneth let Jake and Justin in, and then I walked down the stairs first, followed by Brooke. My dress swishes and sways and lightly dusts each step as I slowly walk down, down, down into Jake's awaiting arms!

"Wow, Gracie! You look incredible!" and he kisses my cheek and gives me a quick one-armed hug, then with the other hand brought up a box with the most delicate and gorgeous wristlet I've ever seen! (Okay, so I've only seen a few in movies, but still this one is GORGEOUS). It has three soft pink roses nestled in sprigs of eucalyptus and teeny white flowers—not sure what they are—with a beautiful sparkly soft pink ribbon! It smells divine.

"Oh, thank you, Jake! It's so pretty and it smells divine!" And it's then that I look back up at him and see how amazing he looks! He rented a tux for tonight and got a matching pale pink bow tie and cummerbund, and holy moly does he ever look freaking good-looking! Like, how can that even be possible? Even better looking than he already is? SHEESH! Be still, my heart! Then Brooke comes down, and the three of us watch in awe as she descends like a queen in her palace!

Justin grins ear to ear and places Brooke's wristlet onto her teeny arm. She kisses Justin, and then our entourage follows Jake, and we head towards Brooke's Candy Red Mustang. The boys help us both in, and we head to Rocky's Steak House.

Our meal is so delicious! Oh my goshhhh! And expensive as crap but worth every penny!! Jake and Justin go with the steak that comes with Rocky's signature mashed red potatoes and baby asparagus. Brooke orders the filet mignon that comes with a potato, carrot, and pea mixture—sounds crazy, but it's super yummo. I've had it before. I go with the catfish. It's my fave. It's lightly breaded in cornbread and comes with this amazing coleslaw. We stuff ourselves—it's a gourmet-ish restaurant, but everything is so flavorful and filling—so not so gourmet that you want to eat a hamburger right after, haha. Each couple decides to share the brownie and blondie combo dessert with chocolate ganache and vanilla ice cream. Bill pays, then the four of us get up to go and see Clara and her boyfriend and their group. We chit-chat for a few minutes, then tell them we will see them at the dance. We four then walk into the beautiful night air, holding hands with our respective significant others, and reach Brooke's red Mustang, piling in once again. This time headed to my very first and last Prom!

I've dreamt of taking a prom picture, too, and that dream came true, too! We took a whole bunch, and that was so fun with all the props they had for us to choose from!

The Prom Committee researched a really great DJ, and the music is incredible! There are intermittent slow dances, but not too many. In fact, my shoes came off immediately 'cause you can't jump dance with dang heels on! But the very last dance is a slow one. They pull out an oldie but goodie 80s slow song—'The Promise' by When In Rome—my parents were 80s kids, and we three kids are very 80s music indoctrinated! Jake takes my hand and leads me to the dance floor. I mean, I get chills up and down my spine like it's the first time he's held my hand! The lights are dim, and I close my eyes and rest my head on his shoulder. As we sway and slowly turn in sync to the song, I imagine I'm in a scene of a movie, and it's as if we're the only two on the dance floor. It's so freaking romantic, I want to explode with happiness! As the song ends, Jake softly places his hands on my cheeks and lifts my head and he leans in and gives me the most fabulous kiss! The tingles fly through my body like fireworks on July Fourth! I don't even remember much about the drive home after that dance OR the kiss 'cause I feel like I'm floating on a cute baby cloud through the sky. Jake walks me to the door, and I give him a huge hug, then push back so I can look into his ocean-blue eyes and thank him.

"Well, Jake, thanks soooo much. That was hands down one of our best date nights EVER!" I say exuberantly.

"Ha ha, you're so cute! But I totally agree. Thanks for being my beautiful date." He leans in and kisses my cheek so softly it's like a butterfly is fluttering right by me.

"Sleep well, whoever gets up first can text, how about?" Jake suggests.

"Absolutely (this is my new go-to word idk why, I just really like it!)," I respond softly and open the door with my hand behind my back, and slowly back into my house, waving goodbye to the three of them. I feel deliriously happy. The house is quiet as it's nearly 1 am. I tiptoe upstairs as quietly as I can and enter my room. I immediately fling off my shoes—but stay in my dress. Definitely Cinderella after the ball vibes flowing through this girl. I lie on my back for a good ten minutes before I turn over onto my stomach and grab my trusty journal to write about tonight.

How can I even put this night into words?

I start by stapling my prom ticket to a clean page, and I also have a Polaroid prom picture they took (I paid for it) of Jake and me, in a frame on my side table. It was such a dreamy night! I carefully take off my wristlet after I'm done explaining every last detail about the night to my trusty journal and hang it on the side of my long mirror. I'll let it dry out, and then I can look at it every day. I slowly go through my bedtime routine, but I want to still gaze at my dress! Okay, I know, nerd alert, but I felt like a fairy princess all night long, so I decided to hang my dress on the front of my closet door, and I carefully covered it with the clear cover that came with it. I'll leave it there for a bit so I can be reminded of a really fantastic Prom night!

Hands down best night ever! I figured I'd never go to prom, and then Jake came into my life, and all the things I have always dreamed of continue to come true—I am giddy with happiness. One more week of April and it's straight into May: finals and graduation!

I turn on my fave Spotify playlist and let the music permeate my happy thoughts.

"OKAY, I CANNOT BELIEVE IT'S ALMOST THE END OF APRIL. I'M freaking out right now!" Brooke says in her normal dramatic tone. It's the Tuesday after Prom weekend. We're in the library together, packing up our backpacks after finishing our third study sesh this week, all of us expressing how much we are ready for the weekend.

But I do agree with her.

"Right? I mean, is it just me, or has this been the fastest year yet? I can't even believe that in four weeks we graduate!" I chime in with Brooke.

"For real!" Justin agrees with us girls. Both he and Brooke got into Pepperdine in California and will be leaving us in June to find housing and jobs.

They'll stay with Brooke's Aunt Mary while they work out that stuff.

"Guys! Let's go! I'm starving and need a bedtime snack!" Beth says exasperatedly.

Everyone turns to her and busts up laughing.

"Okay, already. I'm ready! Everyone, let's go!" Jake says, and we follow him out to his Rubicon.

"Bye Brooke! Bye Justin! Oh, are we doing anything this weekend together?" I call across the parking lot.

"I'll text you guys!" Brooke yells back.

"Cool! See ya tomorrow!" I shout.

Seatbelted in, Jake starts up his Rubicon, and we four head for home.

Jake and I always hold hands while driving in his car, so I reach over to take his hand, and I feel very content with my life right now.

I glance out my window and think happy thoughts while the tunes play, and we four enjoy our ride home together.

I'm so grateful that Jake is cool about driving us everywhere. Especially since Mom sold Ol' Blue, my truck, last summer, 'cause there were too many cars and not enough drivers. Zac took his car, but since both Kenneth and my mom have cars, I take one of theirs whenever I need to go somewhere alone. Now, the driveway is empty and both cars fit in our garage.

So, having him drive us is a plus. I am happy for my good friends, Brooke and Justin. For my fabulous boyfriend, Jake.

For my amazing little sister, Beth, and her best friend, Meg. *Life is feeling good and safe again. Phew! Am I glad?*

Things were out of control for quite a while. I can finally think clearly.

Okay, yeah, it still sucks that Jake and I will be living two hours apart for the first and second year of college, but we can handle it.

I mean, I'm pretty sure we can handle the long-distance thing. I know it won't be easy, but it's what it is, and I need to suck it up and deal with it (I can say this now after some good therapy sessions).

It's true. Emotionally, I feel more stable.

Speaking of stable, I'm surely glad I gave Jake my therapist's info for Meg. She's been gone to see Cindy a few times this month.

"Gracie? Are you okay?" I jolt at Jake's voice. I turn to him.

"Actually, I couldn't be better! I was just reminiscing over the past few months! What a wild ride we've all been on—but I feel things are calm now. I mean, besides your mom being gone, but I mean it has calmed down the stress in your household, I'm assuming?" I say happily as I follow Beth and Meg with my eyes as they walk towards our front door.

Ice cream sandwich time again!

Jake smiles. "Absolutely better—do I miss my mom? Every day. Do I miss their fighting? Not one bit. Meg is doing better. I'm feeling way less stressed, so yeah. I agree with you Gracie. Things have chilled out, and I feel we can slide into graduation with minimal issues."

"For real!! We are sooooo close!! I can't believe it!!" I lean in and give Jake a tender kiss on his lips.

Jake pulls back and looks into my eyes, that I've just fluttered open. I love to kiss Jake. A lot.

"I don't think I say this, like, ever to you, Gracie, but I love to kiss you!" Jake says to me and grins his heart-melting smile.

"Uh, wow, nope, you've not shared that with me. I guess I hoped I wasn't a lame kisser, but I figured you'd tell me? Idk how that's supposed to work, but thanks. You know how I feel about kissing you, I'd imagine! Top five fave things!" I smile, "See you in the morning!! I love the weekend more and more, don't you?" I grin.

Jake smiles back. "Yup! It's been great to have weekends to catch up on sleep and spend time together. Oh, don't forget to text on our group chat about possible plans with Brooke and Justin, okay? I would, but you're much better at planning things. I just need to work on some homework on Saturday morning, but Friday night and Saturday afternoon, I'm open. And your mom asked us over for family dinner on Sunday. My dad, too. So, I think we'll be at your house around four o'clock."

"Oh yeah, thanks for the reminder. Let me put that in my reminders app." I do this quickly—otherwise, I will forget. "I'm glad you all are coming for dinner. And I'm with ya on doing homework to be done on Saturday morning. Hey, also, should we invite Meg and Beth either to hang with us tomorrow night or Saturday?"

"Oh yeah, great idea. Either one," he says.

I nod. "Okay, I'll ask Beth, and she can text Meg. Ah, here comes Meg with her ice cream sandwich treat for the ride home. She kills me! She's so funny! See you tomorrow morning!"

"I know. Meg is so silly," he laughs. "See you and Beth in the a.m.!"

I get out of the Rubicon, close the door, high-five Meg as she walks past me to the passenger side, and go into my house.

My house will always be my safe place. I love it.

The warmth here is because of the love my parents cultivated long ago, and now my mom and Kenneth are doing the same thing.

I am confident that, no matter what future hard times may come our way, we can handle them together.

1 1

MAY (GRADUATION)

"MOMMMMMM! HELP!"

"Gracie, where are you?" she calls back.

"Upstairs! In my room!"

I hear my mom tramp up the stairs.

"What is going on, darlin'?" Mom sweeps into my room. She brings with her an amazing scent cloud of her perfume—I always love her smell—and she looks AMAZING in her LBD (little black dress).

I, on the other hand, can't get my robe to stay put over my new dress, and graduation is happening in less than two hours!

Our high school got the midday shift—eleven o'clock—but we need to be there an hour earlier.

My dress is black and fitted. Not my usual MO. So I am not very mobile in it! I'm also wearing a chunky-heeled dressy sandal—also not my MO, but when you go shopping with Brooke, you better be prepared to go with whatever she throws your way.

And for me, she suggested a fitted LBD and chunky-heeled sandals.

"Okay, how can I help?" Mom asks.

"Are there wrinkles in the robe? Is it lying right? I feel a bit awkward in this dress and these heels. Help!" I plead.

83

"Turn towards me, please." She uses her *mother's magic* and fiddles here and there with me.

"Now, what do you think?" she asks.

I turn back around and check myself out. "Ahhh, thanks, Mom! Phew. Hope about my hair? Makeup?"

"Stunning. Your hair looks beautiful. It's grown so much this year. I like the longer length. And yes, your makeup looks wonderful. You really lucked out having Brooke as a friend. She's a good teacher of all things fashionable!" Mom smiles her wide, warm smile at me.

"Agreed. Thanks, Mom. Okay, Jake is coming to pick me up in like five minutes. Then you guys take off in about forty-five minutes—don't forget your tickets—and find seats. We will be down on the floor. Then, Jake's family, our family, and Brooke and Justin's families are all meeting at one-thirty p.m. at Lupe Tortilla. They've got our reservations. Brooke's dad took care of it all. Thankfully, one less thing for us kids to worry about. Love ya, Mom. Thanks for your help."

I grab my purse, give mom a hug and a cheek kiss, and try not to fall as I descend the stairs.

"See you in a bit then! Love ya back, Gracie girl." I hear her words as I get a text from Jake.

Jake <here>

Grace <ready coming>

As I come out of my house, I see Jake is on the passenger side. My door is open.

Cute boy. I'll take the help today.

"Hi! You look awesome. So handsome," I trill. "Thanks for getting the door! My independence is slightly marred by this outfit!" I laugh, and Jake helps me into his Rubicon.

"Well, you look hot if that counts for anything!" He grins.

I blush and smile.

Jake goes around, hops in the Rubicon, and puts it into reverse as he backs us out of my driveway.

"This is it, Today's the day! We made it!" he says to me with his beautiful smile, and crinkles appear around his blue eyes, which are always swimmable!

"I know! I KNOW!! I can't believe it. Today is a legit, unique day! A day that signifies we're growing up, moving forward, and all that. Wow, wow, wow." I settle myself in the seat as best as I can.

At least my dress is knee-length and not too short, ha-ha. I didn't want to worry about that issue! I know—dramatic!

Jake and I arrive at the stadium (in Texas, everything is bigger, even the size of graduating classes, so we use stadiums or large church venues for graduations). We were told to check in and then get into groups according to our last names, which meant that I went one way and Jake went another. We kiss each other quickly and find our assigned areas.

Everyone is then checked in once again, and we proceed to file into the chairs set up in the middle of the field. The parents and family members will start arriving soon to find a seat—there will be a lot of people here today, as our graduating class has 150 seniors. Once we are all seated, I crane my neck to see if I can find Jake. I'm M for Miller, and he's H for Hansen, so we're quite a ways away from each other.

I finally find him. He's standing and shading his eyes as if he's looking for something or someone. Our eyes meet—me! He is looking for me! I wave and he reciprocates. Then, we hear over the mic that it's time for everyone to take their places. So, everyone attempts to quiet down. Commencement will start in 30 minutes. The weather is cooperating. Thankfully. You never know with Texas!

I'm never going to find my family, so I don't even try. As long as they get footage of Jake and I when we walk, and also Brooke and Justin, then I will be satisfied. I glance at the program. A welcome, two speakers from our graduating class, then the reading of the graduates. Our Valedictorian speaks, as per tradition. She's a great person. She'll be attending Rice—you go girl! The next speaker is our class president. Thankfully, he is a good guy, too. He'll be attending Vanderbilt in Nashville.

I'm going to try and not feel like a little lost flea on a dog's fur who doesn't know which way is up! I am confident in my choice, and will be reapplying in a semester anyway, so it's all good. IS IT ALL GOOD? Nope. Done. No revisiting. This is your graduation day. ENJOY YOURSELF GRACIE! NO TIME FOR LOW SELF-ESTEEM CRAP!

The Vice-Principal, Mr. Bean (yeah, get it all out of your system, 'cause he's heard all the jokes!) begins reading the names. It's going to take a long while....

"Jacob Lee Hansen," I jump up from my chair, attempting not to twist my ankle in my new shoes. I scream and shout! He looks so beautiful. I am so proud of him, of us, all of us.

"Brooklyn Kate Marchant," I scream and cheer! I am also lining up 'cause my name is coming up soon.

"Grace Lou Miller." I hear yelling and screaming and horns, but I don't dare look, so I don't trip as I ascend the three stairs. I walk slowly and carefully. I then walk across the stage, shake all the hands, and descend on the other side—phew!! I made it! (Luckily, we did practice in our elective classes a few times—so that was a plus.)

As I return to my row and chair, I see my family! I give them all an excited wave. I'm barely back in my chair when Justin's name is called.

"Justin David Nelson," and I am standing and wildly cheering and screaming yet again! I love our little group of friends!

Jake, Brooke, Justin, and I plan to meet by a tree on the north side of the stadium for pictures and to gather before we go and eat.

My thoughts suddenly steer me to my dad. It's these types of occasions that make me miss him so very much; it hurts my soul. I swallow hard and put the painful thought into a safe place in my mind and heart. Something to revisit later when I write in my journal tonight.

The last name is called, and Principal Stanley ends the ceremony with a beautiful and encouraging send-off:

"Remember who you are; don't ever forget where you want to go and what you want to become. Be strong and make good choices! Move your tassels from one side to the other! Congratulations! And now here is your new graduating class from San Pasqual High School!"

Screaming! Yelling! Tears! Hugs galore! Hats thrown up and caught! And then I must somehow get through this crowd and outside the doors to my group! Good luck to me, ha-ha.

I feel like a sardine rolled into that weird rectangular container they come in. I'm shoulder-to-shoulder with fellow classmates on both sides. I just go with the flow of students, and after 20 minutes, I see the light of the doors! I made it! I turn left out of the stadium and see my friends, Jake, and our families all coming together. Jake's mom couldn't make it, but they FaceTimed earlier this morning, so that was a positive for Jake.

"Mom! Kenneth! I'm here!" I yell as I near them.

They give me a double hug, one after the other.

"We are so proud of you, sweet girl, so proud." I beam with what can only be utter joy!

Picture after picture is taken until finally Beth is done!

"Okay, don't mean to be a party pooper and break up this whole shindig, but can we please go and eat now?? I'm gonna die of actual starvation!" Beth says with obvious drama, which makes us all chuckle, since she's never dramatic, so she must be REALLY starving.

"Of course! Everyone knows where we are meeting? Lupe Tortilla. Off the tollway," Mom tells everyone.

Jake and I climb into his jeep, and everyone else into their own cars, and we take off for the restaurant. It's about 20 minutes away. The music is on. Jake and I are holding hands and enjoying the drive together.

What a great day! Really, though, it has been so wonderful. I only thought about my dad once during the graduation ceremony. I was thinking that my dad would have been super proud of me and my friends. And I often think about what he'd think about Jake and me dating. I know he'd like Jake. But probably wouldn't be his favorite to see that I was dating one boy exclu-

sively, because he's a dad, but I do believe he would be eventually okay with it all.

By the time we all arrive at the restaurant just before 2 pm, we are both starving *and* exhausted.

The parents all sit together, obviously, and all of us teens sit together at another table.

Everyone orders their drinks and some appetizers to share, and then begins a beautiful buzz of happy conversation as we all eat.

I look around the table and try to soak in everyone's face so I can remember this day. I can literally feel so much love surrounding me like a warm blanket. I love these people so much!

Then my thoughts take me straight to all of the memories of where we all were and where we've ended up on this day. As Jake, Brooke, Justin, and I have now finished this chapter of our lives, I am glad we have all been able to support one another over the past year, and for Jake and me, the past two years.

We will definitely all stay in touch. ALSO, as we finish this chapter of our young lives, there will be A LOT of changes!

Brooke and Justin will be leaving by the end of June. Ugh. That's so soon! And then—be still my heart—Jake will leave mid-August. Yes, I know he'll only be a couple of hours away, but not seeing each other every day will be weird.

Anyway, I'm pushing any negative thoughts to the very back of my brain 'cause Jake and I get the summer together, and for this I can't hardly wait! June, July, and well, I guess half of August. Hallelujah! I mean, yes, we will be working and all, but no school to interrupt us hanging out together. That's what I'm looking forward to.

I shake my head a bit and tune back into the conversations happening all around me, and take another bite of my enchilada dish. It's so good! I love it! As I'm chewing, I hear Meg say something about an art class. My ears perk up because my mom found a brochure for the city of Katy and had me look at some of the courses and activities they offer throughout the year. One is a long list of local art classes with a variety of levels, too. I told my mom I'd think about it, and tbh, I have actually been giving it a lot of thought.

Why did I perk up when Meg mentioned an art class? Is this something I should look into further? I don't need to sign up until the beginning of August, though, so I'll put it on my reminder list for July and revisit the idea. It might just be the thing I need to distract me and help me to learn a new skill.

"Hey, you, why are you so quiet?" Jake asks me with a kind smile.

"Oh, ha, I'm good. I'm great in fact! Well, besides eating, I have been looking at everyone here today. These are all of my people. I love everyone here. I love how much things have changed for the good over the last almost two years. I was thinking that Brooke and Justin are leaving way too soon, but I'm happy for them. I was thinking of us having the majority of our summer to work and hang out together, and I was thinking of taking an art class in the fall," I say to Jake.

"Wait, what? That could be very cool for you. And would be something to really take you out of your comfort zone, don't you agree?" Jake's eyes twinkle as he says this to me.

"Yeah, I think it may. I overheard Meg say something about taking an art class next year, and my ears perked up. Taking that as a sign that it may be something I need to try and see where it goes." I agree with Jake.

Jake leans over and plants a delicate kiss on my lips.

"You're a good person, Gracie Lou, and I'm privileged to be your boyfriend!" Jake says to me, and I instantly blush.

"Oh, it's me who is grateful for you every single day! For real!" I squeeze his hand under the table, and we both turn back to our food and join in with the others and the ongoing conversations.

12

JUNE-JULY

"OH MY GOSH! HELLOOOOO EVERYONE!!" I say loudly, smiling ear to ear, as I enter Sicily's Take and Bake Pizza.

I am working a 10:00 a.m. to 7:00 p.m. shift today.

This shift is a lot, because you don't close or open, but work out on the floor making food the entire day.

Shaun and Julie rotate the longer shifts so that everyone gets them once a week, thankfully. It's a bit brutal.

I've been back at work for a few weeks.

After graduation, I met up with Shaun, and he brought me up to speed on their new menu items, some new protocols, and so forth.

Good thing Trevor and James are older to help their momma. And see if we need any supplies. I love it when Julie pops in. Oh! Speaking of, there she is right now!

"Gracie Lou! I am sooooo glad to see you!!" Julie embraces me in a warm momma hug. I love this lady.

"I sincerely missed you so much! Oh, let me see this baby! He's so big now, I can't believe how much he's grown." I coo to Chance and tickle under his chin as he giggles.

"He's huge. I think he's a few pounds bigger than both Trevor and

James at this age. He will turn one at the end of August. I can't believe it either. Time flies when you're living a crazy life!"

We both laugh at her words.

"Okay, I'm here for just a few minutes. What do we need? I'll go by Sammy's Club after I take the boys to the splash pad park today and get what y'all need." She takes out her phone while trying to distract Trevor and James from running around her in circles, trying to tag each other.

"Let me grab the list from Shaun—he's in the back room - be right back. Hey, Trevor, come back with me, will ya? I need your help." I take his tiny hand, and he follows me. Trevor is almost eight, and James will be five.

"Daddy!" Trevor runs to his dad and hugs him on his leg. *So sweet.*

Shaun smiles. "Hey, Trev, are you here with Mom? Here's the list, you guys! Tell Julie thanks. I'm making the pizza dough right now, or I'd come out!"

"No problem, I'll tell her! Let's go Trevor." Trevor follows me back out into the store with the paper list in his hand.

"I saw daddy, mommy!" Trevor shows his mom the list.

"Oh, good sweetie!" Julie acknowledges Trevor.

"And Shaun sends you a hello but can't come out cause he's making the pizza dough," I tell Julie.

"Not a problem at all. I'll say "hi" when I come back later on." She smiles. "Okay boys, let's go!" Julie gives me a quick hug, then shoos the two older boys like little ducklings out the door, with baby Chance on her hip still.

I wave to them all and get back to work, but I watch Julie and her boys as they maneuver their way across the parking lot and to her SUV.

I never really think about having kids because I want to get my degree first, start a career, then get married, and then five years later, think about having kids. So, why the stirrings in my heart as I watched Julie and her boys? I chalk it up to being a person who feels a lot of emotions. I mean, who even knows if Jake and I can do this long-distance thing we're about to embark on? *No time to think about marriage and/or kids! Sheesh.*

The day goes by smoothly. I check my phone.

"Seven pm. I'm outta here!" I say laughingly. I love my job and the people I work with, so I'm totes kidding.

"Thanks for your hard work as always. Gracie. See you later tomorrow," Shaun says as I grab my cross-body bag, my lunch box, and three pizzas. Jake got off at 6 pm, so he texted me to say he'd swing by and pick me up.

We're doing an at-home movie marathon with Beth, Meg, Mom, and Kenneth.

I had Shaun make a few pizzas for me to buy and take home earlier. The benefits of where I work are coming in clutch!

Jake <coming into the parking lot>

Gracie <cool, I'm standing outside on the sidewalk>

I hear Jake's Rubicon before I actually see it—one of my favorite sounds.

He pulls up to the curb, and I open the back door to set the pizzas carefully on the seat. Then, I climb into the passenger seat, aka one of my fave places to be.

"Hi, how are you?" I lean over and give him a peck on his cheek.

"Much better now." Jake grins at me. I smile, and then I feel a rush of heat in my cheeks as I begin to blush.

And yep! I still blush whenever Jake says anything like that to me! What a dork I am! Gosh!!

Jake grabs my hand, per our car-riding routine, and I turn up the music.

We've compiled our fave playlist on Spotify and it's soooo good! We fall into a comfortable silence as we head towards my house.

He knows I need to decompress a bit and not talk since I spent the whole day talking to coworkers and customers.

I text Beth and Mom to let them know that we're on our way with the pizzas and to preheat the oven.

Gracie <hey Beth. Jake, and I have three pizzas and are about five minutes from the house. Can you preheat the oven, pretty please >

Beth <totes what pizzas did you get?>

Gracie <veggie with Alfredo sauce, an XL pepperoni, and a Hawaiian>

Beth <perf oven is preheating>

Gracie <*thumbs up*>

I finish texting and turn to look out my window. Summers bring longer days, which I adore.

I can't handle it when it gets so dark so early in the winter months. Spring renews me from winter blues, and summer gives me energy and makes me so happy.

We arrive at the house, and Jake parks in our driveway. He comes around to my side and grabs the pizzas.

The chances of my dropping them are high. I'm so clumsy. I grab my lunch box, purse, and water bottle and close the Rubicon door.

Tonight's movie will be the OG Jurassic Park, 'cause a new Jurassic movie is coming out in July.

I'm so stoked. Well, we all are, 'cause who doesn't like watching freaky dinosaurs roaming the earth again? Ha ha ha.

Mom and I man the pizza cooking. Beth and Meg are in charge of the plates, napkins, and silverware, and Jake and Kenneth are ready to serve the drinks. We like to set it up buffet style on our spacious kitchen counter.

We happily head into the family room for the movie.

Jake and I plop down into our favorite spot on the large sectional couch. Mom and Kenneth sit beside each other, and Meg and Beth make comfy pillow beds on the floor. In the summer days, I aim to soak in every ounce of time spent with Jake. I take his hand in mine.

I love to hold his strong hand. I take peeks at his handsome face from time to time in the darkened room—he is such a good person.

My heart aches for him, too, because his mom has made a huge rift in their family. This breaks my heart! I feel sorry for all of them, including his mom.

I hope she gets her crap together one day. Jake and Meg FT her and text. But they haven't seen her irl since she moved back to Cali. Sucks. That's for sure.

Jake's hands are rough as he has been working at the mechanic shop again. We were both lucky to snag our previous jobs from before our senior year. I know this rarely happens. On Sundays, I use that Aquaphor stuff and rub it on his hands to help offset the dryness and calluses.

Though it doesn't bother me one bit that his hands are slightly rough, instead, it makes me proud of him. I'm proud of the fact that he works hard and even cares about working and saving money.

No offense to Zac's fiancée, Sarah, but she grew up wealthy. She is a little too princessy for me sometimes. But she's kind and loves and adores Zac, so that's all I care about.

Along with soaking in my time with Jake, I've done a lot of thinking about what it would be like not to be together every day.

I am working with my therapist, too, and have some calming exercises. I am looking into some hobbies and things like that. I'm going to spend a lot of time with Beth and probably Meg, too.

And I'll have my classes, of course. It's not like I can't survive without a boyfriend. I never thought this would happen in my life. I wasn't emotionally prepared for what it would be like to date someone I adore. And then to know that that person will be gone for me.

And yeah, we can FaceTime or text. We can call—all that good stuff—but there's something about spending time with a person one-on-one that makes life enjoyable, fun, and happy.

So, this is why I'm soaking in all of this: soaking in his facial expressions, soaking in his laugh, and soaking in how it feels to hold hands.

As we continue watching the movie and Alan herds the kids to safety, it makes me think of my dad. Missing him, missing his face, missing his hug, missing the time we had together.

And I think that's why I'm getting a little emotional, and that's what my therapist just talked to me about.

I guess there's a sort of abandonment-like feeling that comes with having a parent pass away, and I think Jake is feeling this too, as he mentioned to me the other day about his mom being gone.

It makes him think about being away from me, too. Who knew there were so many emotions involved with all of this? I certainly did not.

I was not emotionally prepared for my dad to die. Then again, I don't know who could ever be prepared for that. Jake most likely wasn't emotionally prepared for his mom to leave. And then come back, and then leave again.

I have such big emotions, that's why I've seen a therapist for the last five years. She has helped me to emotionally regulate, which means getting my emotions under control and not letting them rule my day or situation.

It's been very hard.

A velociraptor leaps out at Ellie, scaring us all. I reflect on how life can sometimes be like that.

It was like when Brooke moved in, and I literally couldn't handle her on any given day. I had zero patience for her. I hated the way she treated me. I hated the way she flirted with Jake. I just have a lot of emotions that I have been learning to "regulate," which is the therapy word, and so I've been working on that. To regulate.

Sometimes I wish I were more like Jake, Mom, and Zac. And I could regulate my emotions easily, and I didn't have to worry about things building up in my mind and heart. But it's fine in the sense that I can work on it.

Beth is completely the opposite of me. She keeps everything she feels deep inside of her. She doesn't communicate a lot, and she is also learning. She and I have had some killer discussions this summer about how to let her emotions out. And she's helped me to keep my emotions in check.

It's been cool to learn from my little sister.

Zac and my mom are always very chill. Emotionally, they're always level. It makes me feel like the black sheep of the family.

The Tyrannosaurus rex roars as a banner for the park flutters to the floor in front of him.

Jake looks over at me, and I smile, trying to pull myself back into the here and now and enjoy the moment.

My mind wanders again, however. As I said, I continue to work on emotional regulation. And it's working. This will all help me as Zac and Sara continue to be away. And as Jake moves on to college.

I mean, let's remember how upset I was when Jake got in and I didn't get into UT Austin. I tend to let my feels get in the way of any logic or sanity.

I actually wish I could be like a robot sometimes and not feel any feelings.

It's really annoying sometimes. My brain makes up stories that COULD be but aren't! I'm working on it, though!

Anyway, I went off on an emotional tangent, but it was an important detail to share because of all the feelings I tend to experience and am currently feeling, and will continue to feel. We finished the movie before 11 pm, and since I had been on edge with all of my crazy thoughts, I'm emotionally exhausted and ready to go home.

On the way home in the car, I feel Jake look at me multiple times, wanting to say something, but for some reason, he never does. I know he knows something is up; he's obviously NOT an idiot, but I pretend not to notice that he's looking at me. And ask him questions about which parts were his favorite parts of the movie we saw, in the hopes of keeping myself distracted. As soon as Jake drives into my driveway, I jump out and meet him around the front of his jeep to walk me to the door. I don't want to talk about anything right now until I've sorted through all of my feelings, so I continue to "put on a smiley face" and pretend like everything is smooth like butter on toast.

Jake always gives me a huge hug and a cheek kiss every time he drops me off at home. He's so sweet. I love his hugs. He's strong and always feels so warm—I know that's goofy, but it's true.

"Thanks for a great night! I love those movies. I'll text ya tomorrow after church." I say it rapidly and am in the door, closing it as quickly as lightning.

I trudge up the stairs and say goodnight to Beth, Mom, and Kenneth. Sunday tomorrow. Church this year starts at 10:30 am, so that we can sleep in a bit. I grab my journal. Like I said, I've been doing a lot of pondering in preparation for NEXT MONTH when Jake will leave to go to Austin.

I pop in my AirPods and let my favorite playlist melt away any stress or worry as I write down all I've been feeling for the past few weeks: ideas to help me cope. Ideas to stay connected with Jake. Ideas to do with Beth. I also need to register for my classes this month. Oh! I will start volunteering at the food pantry myself in September.

The staff will train me on how to intake new clients. I am very stoked for this. Thus far, we four (Jake, I, Brooke, and Justin) have done checking and sorting, so being able to expand my skill set is exciting for me.

This was one goal my therapist suggested to me: to volunteer somewhere, by myself. Then, find a hobby. I'm still working on that, ha-ha.

I start writing everything down, and before I know it, an hour has passed.

I quickly wash my face, brush my teeth, and finally drop into bed well after midnight—but it was worth it to spend time with my people tonight and to write in my journal!

13

AUGUST

"Okay, I think I got everything on my list," I tell Jake as I drop the items into his cart.

"Cool, thanks, Gracie. I just need a pillow, a desk lamp, and a few more school supply items. Let's head to the school supplies aisle," he tells me.

"Sweet. Let's go!" I am walking beside the cart as Jake pushes it. We've been out doing errands literally all day.

I took the day off (it's a Saturday) so I could help get the rest of the stuff he needs, and help him pack tomorrow after church. Jake plans to leave on Monday!

ARGH! Less than two days left together! I've had a lump in my throat threatening to make me cry at any moment for the last week or so, but I've kept my emotions in check, thankfully. I don't want to be a Debbie Downer for Jake, so I've kept myself busy, happy, and I've been as helpful as I can be to Jake and my family.

"Look! A two-pack. Always a good idea, I say!" I grab the two packs of pillows as Jake gives me a thumbs up and throw them into the cart.

We make our way toward the front of the large warehouse store. "Anything else while you're here?" I ask him.

"Yeah, actually. I think I'll stock up on bar soap, maybe a first aid kit, and some headache meds and body wash."

"Good idea. Then you won't have to buy toiletries each week. That stuff adds up way too fast."

"Totally. Sheesh." Jake says.

We cruise down the toiletry aisles:

Bar soap. Check.

Body wash. Check.

First aid kit. Check.

Headache meds. Check.

We throw everything into the cart as we find what he needs and head toward the checkout.

Jake has an apartment with three other dudes. They have already been texting each other. Two are from Texas, and one is from California. They are great guys.

They all have meal plan cards since Jake and his roomies don't want to have to cook this year. They'll just stock up on snacks and breakfast stuff for the apartment, which reminds me to ask Jake if he wants any bulk snacks while we're still here.

"What about snack stuff? Want to get anything while we're still here?" I ask.

"Oh yeah. Duh. Good idea. Let's head toward the protein bars and drinks section, then I'll grab some cold cereal." Jake grabs a few different boxes of bars, then two boxes of Mister Muscle milks as he wheels toward the cold cereal aisle.

"Which ones would you like?" I point.

"Grab Honey Nut Cheerios and bunches of oats. Please."

I do so and put those into the cart, too. "Okay. Do you have your list? Let's double-check to make sure you're good to go." I smile at Jake, and he smiles back at me.

"Thanks for helping me out today. And coming with me. Let me check the list." He runs through the list and checks things off on his phone. "Okay. We got everything. Let's head to my house to unload it all, and then what say we go get some dinner together?"

"I'd love that!" I reply.

For the second time, we head toward the checkout area, having now found all the items Jake will need.

His school doesn't start for a week from Monday, but he needs to get books, unpack, and attend some first-year orientation activities, among other things.

As much as I would love him to stay here for one more week, I need to let him go.

He needs to get himself situated to start the semester off on a strong note. He's a good student and has good study habits, so I'm not worried about that.

But college is way different than high school. That's for sure. Larger classes. Way more work and harder work.

After we unload his car and put everything in the front room, where his other belongings are, we check in with his dad and Meg.

"Dad?" Jake calls.

"Here, son. In my office. I'll come to you." His dad appears around the corner and heads down the hallway to the front room area. "Hey, Gracie. Good to see you today."

"Hey, Mr. Hansen. You too!" I smile.

"Where's Meg?" Jake asks.

"With Beth. I dropped them off at an early movie," Mr. Hansen says.

"Okay, cool. Gracie and I are going to get some dinner. Want to come with us?" Jake asks his dad.

Mr. Hansen nods. "You know, I'd love that. I'll follow you two. Where do you want to eat?"

"The Torchy Tortilla!" we both say in unison.

Jake's dad laughs. "Not surprised. K. Let me get my keys and wallet, and I'll meet you both there."

"Sounds good, Dad," Jake says, and he takes my hand and leads me out the front door and to his Rubicon.

I climb into my side, and he does the same on the driver's side. As we back up, I watch as the garage opens and his dad pulls out.

How I hate that his wife is gone. And that their divorce is almost final. It breaks my heart for all of them. It super sucks.

I wish Daphne could have figured out how to be a mother and wife. She just can't do it. I wish I understood why. It's hard for me to be forgiving of her since I've got a stellar mom who's always there for me. Always.

I feel awful for Jake and Meg most of all. Which kid doesn't want a mother who's there and supportive of them? I mean, I think every kid does. Unless the mother is a jerk, but that's rare.

Jake keeps up with his mom. They text and sometimes FaceTime. She sent him two pairs of sheets and a cool duvet cover set for his bed at his new apartment. That was really cool because it would have been expensive if Jake had to buy that too, along with everything else he's been buying.

Sigh. Maybe . . . Daphne will wise up? Come back home for good? Idk what I want her to do, but being so far away is difficult for all three of them.

Jake says it breaks his heart, but he's working through it. Meg has been going to my therapist this summer, and it's making a big difference. Jake also shared with me. I'm so glad. This stuff is rough to work through, accept, and deal with. I know how it is.

I've lived it and still live it. *Your heart just hurts and hurts and hurts, and you feel like it will never stop hurting!*

And then one day, it starts to feel not AS painful. And another year passes. Then, the pain lessens further. Anyway, I'm glad Jake is okay and that Meg is getting the help she needs. *So much to deal with in this life!*

Dang. It sometimes drives me crazy to the point that I really feel I can't handle these tough times.

Ugh. It gets to be too much. Too hard. Too hurty. Too awful. Then, before I knew it, I was on the other side of it all, and I survived!

And I'm then able to help others, just as I've been doing with Meg. This makes me feel strong. It makes me feel capable.

If only I could remember these thoughts when I am GOING THROUGH hard situations. Ha! What am I saying to myself?

Duh, Gracie. I can put that to the test starting Monday! Fingers crossed I can handle it and survive....

At the end of our meal, I see Mr. Hansen, aka Samuel, call Meg and Beth over. They were sitting together at the end of our table.

Then, he gave them the keys, and I watched as they both walked out laughing and talking.

"So, I want to talk with you both for a little bit. The girls will turn on the car and hang out there for a little bit while we talk," Mr. Hansen says. He looks sad and puts his head down for a minute. Jake and I glance at each other and shrug.

"So, I met your mother in high school, you know the story, right, Jake?" Mr. Hansen begins.

"Yeah, Dad, of course. Senior year. Mom moved in, and you were smitten from the moment you saw her, but didn't date until after you both graduated high school. And the rest is history, as they say, 'cause you married a few years later."

"Yep, so that's why I wanted to talk with you both. You've been dating for a while now, and I see that you both seem very compatible—your mother and I were that way too—and then she changed. I've gone over it all in my head a million times, wondering if there was something different I should have done before we got married." Mr. Hansen looks at Jake, then at me. I swallow hard.

I'm hating this all right now. I feel nauseated! What is happening? How are we like him and Daphne? And Jake and I ARE totally compatible. I'm nothing like her. What the actual!

I tune back into the conversation, not feeling very happy about where this conversation is going to end up. Nope. Not happy.

"Dad, " Jake starts to say, but his dad interrupts him.

"Look, Jake, and Grace, I'm not saying your relationship is like ours, but I want you to be sure to both be aware that there are many people to date out there, and just because you're good together now might not mean you'll be good for each other in a few years, is all I'm saying," he finishes.

I say nothing. I can't say anything because I might either scream or cry. It's a toss-up.

I feel Jake tense up next to me. "Thanks for sharing that with us, Dad. We will talk about this all together. I think we'd better go—I need to get Gracie home. Thanks for the meal, Dad, it was delicious." And with that, Jake scoots his chair back and rises, so I do the same and follow Jake out to his jeep. We're both very silent as we get in and buckle up. Jake doesn't even put on any music. I can tell he's fuming, and y'all know how I'm feeling: SO FREAKING MAD! We have a fifteen-minute drive home, so I'm hoping Jake calms down some before he heads home. I'm not sure how he'll talk to his dad when I'm not there. Not great, is what I think. I don't like silence, so I decide to break it.

"Well, that was interesting, I guess is the word I'd use. While I can appreciate what your dad is saying, I, um, I don't know if we're the same as your Mom and Dad. I mean, are we? What do you think?"

Jake scowls. "Yeah, I will be having a big talk with my dad when I get home. I don't feel like that was really very appropriate to have you there, too. Now, if it were just me? Sure, then we could have discussed it at length. But with you there? Son of a biscuit, I'm so ticked off right now."

"Oh shoot, yeah. I figured you weren't really happy about how that had gone down. I felt like flames were coming out of my ears! I'm not trying to be disrespectful to your mom, but I'm nothing like her." I say that in a very soft voice 'cause I'm kind of hoping I'm right and that I'm nothing like her.

"You're not Gracie, and I'm not my dad. Period." Jake whips his jeep into the driveway.

"I'll text you later, okay? Are you cool to walk yourself up?" Jake asks me.

"Yep, not a problem at all. Good luck." I lean over and kiss him on the lips and give him a big hug. Then we both pull back and look at each other for about 30 seconds, after which I jump out, close my door, and head to my front door so that I can go inside my house.

I turn to wave goodbye, but Jake has already backed out and is driving off, so he didn't see me wave.

CRAP. I don't think I've ever seen Jake mad. Like ever! He's been bugged, but not mad. I hope that conversation will end okay, because I'm a little, no, make that A LOT worried.

I head inside and straight to my room. I need to do some serious writing in my journal tonight. This has been a VERY emotional day, and all I can think of is Jake's dad and him and the weird conversation, and that TOMORROW is Jake's last day at home before he leaves to go to college.

And I can't believe he's got to straighten his dad out—that's gonna be awkward and upsetting. I hope it goes better than I'm envisioning it COULD go. And then I can't believe that it's almost here: THE day I've dreaded even though I've been trying to tell myself I'm fine, but I know deep down within me that I've been lying to myself to say that I won't cry and I can handle it and I know I say that I'm fine but I won't be fine at all. I know I'll cry like a little girl whose dolly dropped in the dirt and whose heart is literally broken!

JAKE TEXTED ME A LITTLE BIT AGO. I WAS IN CHURCH, SO I TEXTED HIM right after we got home. Apparently, he and his dad talked and talked, getting a lot out on the table and discussing everything that had been bugging them both for a long time.

I guess there's been way too many unsaid things and stories made up over the last few years between Jake and his dad. BUT they talked and talked, and worked through things enough that they can drive out of here tomorrow getting along. His dad apologized to Jake for being so weird at dinner on Saturday. I was glad to hear this 'cause it was so awkward and maddening at the same time!

Meg and Jake will stop by later tonight to drop off Meg's stuff because she'll stay overnight with us for a few days, since Jake and his dad need to leave by 8 am, and Meg and Beth will already be at school, and they'll need time to get Jake all set up. Which also means Jake is just dropping by and then leaving, because he and his dad need to continue packing his Rubicon so they can swing by my house, say goodbye, and then head out tomorrow morning. I'm trying not to be a selfish git and feel sorry for myself. But let's be honest. It's hard not to want to wallow in self-pity.

"Hey, guys!" I greet Jake and Meg at the door as I hear Jake's jeep pull into my driveway. It's nearly 8:00 pm by the time they get to our house. I can see from my doorway that there's quite a bit of stuff already in the back of his jeep.

"Hey, Gracie," Jake says and leans in and pecks me on the cheek. "I'm sorry to not be hanging with you tonight. I feel bad. I really do."

"Will you please stop worrying? I'm fine. We had a great day together Saturday—well, for the most part." We both laugh. "But really, as long as I can give you a hug and kiss before you head out tomorrow, that will be perfect." What a liar I am, but I smile a sincere smile.

Jake gives me a quick hug and another peck on my cheek, and then, before I can say another goodbye, he's climbing into his jeep and is gone.

I close the front door slowly and head upstairs to my room. I close my door, pop in my AirPods, check my school bag and art bag, and make sure my work uniform is clean and ready.

How the heck am I supposed to relax? Good grief, I feel completely on edge! I need to relax and go to sleep so I'm ready for Jake tomorrow morning.

I end up listening to music for a couple of hours, reorganizing my closet, and cleaning up my room completely. Yeah, you know I'm trying to have time pass as quickly as possible, even when I'm cleaning my room voluntarily.

Finally, it's 10:00 pm and I text Jake to say goodnight. We do this every night now.

Gracie <<hey you hope the rest of your car packing went okay! Sending you good night wishes>>

Jake <<ah thanks sweet Gracie. Yeah, we've got everything in. I'm exhausted,8s heading to bed now. See ya in the am>>

Gracie <<see you tomorrow>>

And then, I turn my light out and tiny tears trickle down my face as I cry myself to sleep.

"THANKS FOR COMING BY, JAKE! I KNOW I'M THE OPPOSITE OF THE WAY you'll be going. I appreciate it, really," I say softly.

"Well, as sweet as that is, I know you'd murder me dead if I didn't come by, 'cause I would do the same thing!" He laughs, and we embrace each other for a long time. Okay, maybe two minutes, but it felt long, and warm and safe.

Then Jake pulls back first, and we look into each other's eyes for a bit before we both lean in for a long kiss. And then he's walking to his jeep. His dad is waiting patiently in the car. And I watch as Jake climbs into his jeep. I need to savor this moment: his face, the hug, the kiss, his smell, all of it, because he won't be able to come home for like three weeks.

And then he's backing out of our driveway, and I'm standing in my driveway. My tears begin to flow freely down my face. I let them fall. I don't even care. I follow Jake's Rubicon and keep waving until it's out of sight. I cover my eyes with my hands.

This is it. It's happened. He's gone....

I wipe my cheeks with the back of my hand and slowly walk to my front door, which is open 'cause my Mom is standing there waiting for me so she can embrace me. I step right into her arms. And I sob like a little girl whose ice cream has fallen off her cone onto the sidewalk.

Mom guides me into the family room, where we both sit side by side on the comfy couch. "Are you okay, Gracie?"

"Yeah, I knew I'd cry, but sheesh. I feel like a water faucet! Jake was so nice to come over and officially say goodbye to me, though. Since I said goodbye last night, which, by the way, was the worst, we both cried. Good grief! It's not like he's going to another country!" I say tearfully.

"It's okay. You both have grown really close to each other. Two years is a long time to date one another and get to know one another. You've spent so much time together, too! You guys knew the saying goodbye part would be the worst of Jake leaving for Austin. But, then again, you never really know how something feels until you experience it for yourself." She put her arm around me.

"True, very true." I sigh and nuzzle my head into her shoulder.

We stayed like this for a little bit, and then I must have ended up closing my eyes and dozing off, because about an hour later, I felt my shoulder being jostled and heard my mom telling me to wake up. "Mom? Did I fall asleep?"

"You sure did! I know you've got work in about an hour, though, so I wanted to be sure you had plenty of time to get ready and make lunch to bring with you." She smiles down at me and motions for my hand, which I hold out so she can pull me up. "Okay, I know you know this, but you've got this. Operation: keep-yourself-busy begins now! Oh! When is your first painting class? I keep forgetting to ask you."

"Oh my gosh! It's tomorrow morning! I nearly forgot. Thanks for the reminder. I'm going to go to the hobby store after work tonight and grab my supplies." I put a reminder in my phone.

"Great idea. Did they give you a list of stuff to purchase for the class?" Mom asks.

I pull the list up on my phone and show her. "Yep! It's a semester-long class that meets twice a week, and I think it's a great value for what I paid. I also get to take it at the Katy Art House downtown. Which is the literal cutest house ever!! Have you seen it?"

"The one that is kitty-corner from the Presbyterian church?" she clarifies.

"Yes! It's so adorable! Colorful, peppy. It makes me so happy whenever I drive by it! And, Shaun is totes cool with me requesting the mornings off on Tuesdays and Thursdays! He's so kind to me, like really kind," I beam.

"He and Julie are gems! That's for sure. I'm super excited for this new adventure for you, too! Who knew you'd be interested in painting? I mean, none of us are painters! Ha-ha." Mom laughs as she says this to me.

"I know, I know, I just felt like it was something I wanted to try, so I went for it! I am excited, a little nervous, but excited, too." I grin.

She smiles back. "I'd feel the same way! Okay, gotta get back to work. And, as you know, Meg will be hanging out at our house today and tomorrow, since Jake's dad went with him to help him set up his apartment."

"Oh yeah, good. That makes me happy for Beth. K. Going to get ready for work. I'm off by 6:00 pm tonight, so I'll text you when I'm leaving to go to the hobby store, okay?" I say.

"Sounds great! Love ya Gracie."

"Love ya, Mom!" I call as I sprint up the stairs. I shower, dress in my uniform of jeans and a Sicily's Take and Bake Pizza t-shirt, put on my well-padded shoes, braid my hair in two braids, and pop on my baseball cap. I apply simple makeup. I grab my backpack and then dash down the stairs to the kitchen to eat something and pack up my lunch and some snacks, and somehow my mind wanders back to a few weekends ago. Remember? When Jake and I and his dad went out to eat, and then that whole awkward conversation broke out, and Jake's dad made us feel like we were making a big mistake to date and stay together and do the long-distance thing? Anyway, Mr. Hansen also apologized to me. I told him it was okay and that I knew he meant well. But he said he was out of line to compare us to him and Daphne. I remember I just smiled and said nothing more, but inside I was shouting YEAH DUH, DUDE!

I grab my backpack and head out the door to work. I grab the keys to my mom's Honda Pilot. She and Kenneth will use his Lexus if needed today, and then my thoughts run away inside my brain once again. Though this time it's my own personal reminder to not be an emotional knucklehead.

I am going to be mature today and NOT wait with bated breath for Jake to text.

He told me he would be super busy all day and would check in with me later this evening. Okay, so not my fave, but I can handle it. Thus, the keeping-myself-busy plan. Plus, I am looking forward to my painting class. I read that my teacher will also teach us basic drawing skills, which I'm really excited about, since I can only draw stick figures at the moment.

I back my Mom's car out very carefully.

Sometimes I miss Ol'Blue because it was old and not fancy. I always felt comfortable in it. These fancier cars give me stress!

My phone pings just as I close the garage door.

I put the car in park in the driveway and applied the brakes to see who it was, hoping it was Jake, but knowing it wasn't.

Brooke <yo, what's up? Did Jake leave already?>

Gracie <Oh my goodness, yes. I cried like a baby>

Brooke <so sorry, sucks. What are you doing today?>

Gracie <heading to work and then getting supplies for my art class, I start tomorrow morning>

Brooke <oh yeah, cool, Justin and I are all moved in, and we found jobs. I am so excited, there's a mall super close and Justin is working at H&M and I'm working at Zara>

Grace < Fabulous, so happy for you guys, I will text you after my class tomorrow>

Brooke <cool ciao>

Gracie <ciao>

My shift flies by, for which I'm always glad.

I love my job, obvi, but today I am chomping at the bit to be done so I can go to Charlie's Art Supplies near my house. And awaiting a text or call from Jake. It's nearly 7:30 pm, and I haven't heard anything from Jake yet.

Just keep focused on your task at hand, Gracie. It's all good. Jake is just busy. Or he'd be texting you.

Luckily, Charlie's doesn't close until 8:30 pm, so I've got time.

I scroll through the notes app on my phone to check my class supply list.

Paint brushes

Gouache and watercolor paint

Paint palette

Mixed media sketchbook

Pencils and a kneaded eraser

Mod Podge spray

Charcoal

Portfolio folder

Canvases

I head towards the paint supplies aisle. I find both the watercolor and gouache paint.

I find the mixed-media sketchpad, along with some pencils and that weird eraser.

The paint brushes are trickier. I look at my list again.

Get sizes 6, 8, 10, and 12 and a pack of smaller brushes—mixed media.

"Good thing I reread the supplies sheet for the third time!!" I say to myself while perusing the paintbrush aisle.

I quickly find every size of brush required and load them into my basket.

This may cost me quite a bit to get started, but I'm ready to dive into something very new and very opposite from what I usually do.

I love to write in my journal, but this is a whole new adventure. Hope to pick up on the drawing and painting skills soonish.

I'm low-key feeling a bit stressed, but it's an excited stress, if that's a thing.

I go to the register to buy my items; the total is $67. Holy.

That is a lot. I have a cute bag at home that I will load all of this stuff into later tonight.

I need to get some rest, too, since class is from 9 am to 11 am, then I'll bop home for lunch and go to work half-day.

I make my way to my car, fling my purchases onto the passenger seat, and walk around to get in and start the car.

PINGGGGGGGGGGG

My heart leaps. *Jake??????*

Jake <gracie lou, I'm alive what a day I just got done right now, getting everything set up, had to go to the hardware store the grocery store and had to unload, unpack and make up my bed and so much more>

Gracie <oh my stars that's a lot of stuff to do wish I could have helped you>

Jake <me too although my dad has been a stellar helper today>

Gracie <that makes my heart happy>

Jake <how was your day>

Gracie <after I blubbered and cried, ha ha, I fell asleep, went to work, and I just got all of my supplies for my art class that starts tomorrow am>

Jake < I am sorry you cried, gracie. But the rest of the day seems awesome. I am super excited to see how this class is for you>

Gracie <me too I'm a little stressed but excited too something new>

Jake <you'll do great. so I'm going to get some grub with my dad rn can I text you goodnight later and then I'll try to call tomorrow>

Gracie <of course have fun and no worries if you can call sweet if not it's all good as long as I know you're okay>

Jake <you are the best>

Gracie <ditto>

Of course, I want to talk to Jake, but this is where I am now: getting a grip on my longing to be with Jake and working on standing on my own two feet as an independent female, which I've always done.

However, I admit that I've become somewhat dependent on Jake. So, this separation is actually a twisted blessing—you know, a good thing coming out of a bad situation.

I start the car and arrive home in about ten minutes. Always grateful that I live close to everything.

I open the garage and ever so carefully pull the Pilot into the garage. I grab all of my stuff and stroll into my house through the inside garage door.

"Mom? Kenneth? Beth? Meg?" I call out everyone's names, ha-ha, to see where everyone is at.

"Kitchen, darlin'," my mom responds.

I cruise into the kitchen and receive hellos and sweet greetings.

"What's for dinner? I'm legit starved!" I say dramatically. I'm channeling my inner Brooke.

"Meatloaf, peas, mashed potatoes, and rolls!" Kenneth says with excitement.

"Have I ever told you, Kenneth, just how much I love your cooking?" I smile and take my place at the table. Mom has already dished a plate for me, so I immediately dig in.

"Hey girlies, how was the day?" I direct my line of sight towards both Beth and Meg.

"We went school clothes shopping!" Beth says with glee.

"Yes, we did, and we scored a lot of stuff today. I'm actually excited to start school in two weeks." Meg smiles as she shares this.

"Lucky girls! Do y'all have your actual school supplies, too?" I ask them.

"Yep," Beth answers.

"We got those yesterday," Meg says.

"Tomorrow is schedule pick-up!" Beth says. "Hoping I get all the classes signed up for."

"Me too," Meg agrees.

"I am sure you will," I answer positively, "Glad you girls are all prepared. It's a nice feeling. Now, you can chill until school actually starts!"

"Yep!" They say in unison.

"Hey, Gracie, did you get your painting supplies and such?" Mom asks me.

"I did. It cost me a lot, but I want to have all that the teacher requested, so I just went for it and bought everything. I'll show you guys after dinner. I need to grab the bag, I'm going to load it all into it anyway after dinner." I say.

"Any word from Jake?" Kenneth asks me.

"As a matter of fact, yes. He just texted as I was about to leave the hobby store. He was so busy today that it was crazy. His dad helped him. They had to go to the hardware store and the grocery store. They also set up his bed with his bedding and everything in his room and the apartment. But they got it all done. And they were just going off to dinner tonight. He sounded good, and he sounded happy." I smile.

"Wonderful!!" Kenneth says.

"Fabulous!" Mom adds.

"He texted me too and says he misses me already!" Meg shares softly.

Everyone gives Meg a reassuring smile, and my mom reaches over to her, putting her hand on her shoulder.

"Jake is such a good brother to you. I'm glad. He's very sweet,"

Mom tells Meg, and she gives my mom a weak smile and brushes away a tiny tear on her cheek.

I decide I'd better change the subject for Meg's sake.

"What's up for you girls for the rest of the week?" I ask brightly.

Beth jumps on the question, also realizing the subject needs to change. "Swim party. B-day party. And we need a few more school clothing items. Shoes specifically. It should be a busy week! Oh, and we've got a movie on Saturday we're going to!"

"Okayyyy, social butterflies, good grief!" I say laughingly.

The girls both smile at me, and then we all finish our dinner in a happy silence.

Everyone pitches in to clean up, wash the dishes, and load the dishwasher. I run upstairs, grab my rotor bag with pockets, and head to the family room.

I spread out my art supplies. My mom comes in to check out my stuff. Kenneth had to take a phone call, and the girls went upstairs to Beth's room to watch a show they both like before getting ready for bed.

"Wow! That is a lot of stuff. Let me check it out!" Mom says with excitement.

I watch as my mom oohs and aahs over my items.

"Well, wow. This is going to be a very cool class. I'm looking forward to hearing all about it tomorrow when you've finished." Mom smiles warmly at me.

"Totes. I'm excited and I'm stressed all at once! But mostly excited. Hopefully, it won't be a class full of already amazing artists. It's supposed to be a beginner's art class. We shall see!" I say sarcastically.

"I'm sure it will be just great, sweetie. Well, I'm going to get ready for bed and read. You good?" Mom asks me. What she means is that with Jake being gone.

"I am actually. I mean, after I basically cried myself to sleep this morning. Ha. I pulled myself together. I had a great day at work, and even though I wanted to text Jake all day long, I resisted. So all in all, for day one I'd give myself a 7/10!" I smile at my mom.

"I agree. Well, have a good sleep. I'll see you before you leave for your art class in the morning, k?" she says.

"Perfect. Love you, mom."

"Love you back, Gracie Lou!" She gives me a hug, then walks out.

I turn to my supplies, still all spread out on the couch, and begin to place them into the various pockets and at the bottom of the bag.

Then I set it by the front door so I won't forget it.

That would suck big time if I started without my supplies. Oh man. That literally makes me so stressed to even think about that happening!!

I check the front door and lock it. Then the back door. Turn off various lights that are still on and then head upstairs to my room.

The door to Zac's room is usually closed, but for some reason it's open. I stop and glance around.

It's hard to be away from those we love. It's really hard.

Sigh. I always miss Zac. Now I get to miss two great guys! Good thing there's texting these days. What if I had to depend on the mail? Pffff. That would make me crazy!

I close his door and continue down the hallway. As I pass Beth's room, I hear them giggling together.

Good. Life for Meg has been anything but simple. First, her mom left, and now Jake is off to college. Blah. She'll make it through this all, I know. But it's good she has Beth. Makes my heart happy for her.

I finally make it to my room. I quickly get on my Jammies, wash my face, brush my teeth, and sit on my bed—time to write out the day's events. Then I need to get to bed!

A pleasant smile stays on my face as I write about sending Jake off, my tears, of course, work, going to the hobby store, and a good evening with my family.

I grab my AirPods, close my journal, and queue up my beach sounds playlist.

Before plugging in my phone to get charged, I want to text Jake a good night message, but my phone pings.

Jake <dinner was great. We're at the hotel together, Dad and I. He'll head home tomorrow. I'm wishing you pleasant dreams, Gracie>

Gracie <thanks Jake, and to you too, glad you're having a great time with your dad>

Jake <freshman orientation stuff all day tomorrow. I can call at dinner time>

Gracie <cool. I'm off work by 6:30 pm!>

Jake <night!>

This is going to be very different for both of us.

Different cities.

Different experiences.

Different classes.

Different schedules.

But it's good because I wasn't looking for a boy to complete me two years ago. *Absolutely not!*

I complete me. Not my boyfriend, but is compatible with who I am.

I have a happy smile on my face as I drift off to dreamland.

SEPTEMBER

IT'S BEEN a month since Jake went away. It's been a month since I started my art class. And it's been a month since the girls started high school.

Zac and Sarah came home for two weeks in August and then returned to college.

Jake and I are now in a good rhythm. We text every day. Check in with each other and share things about our days with one another, too.

We will talk if there's time, but I am respecting his time and vice versa. One thing my dad taught me a while ago was that just because someone doesn't text you back doesn't mean they don't like you. It doesn't mean that they don't care; it just means that they're busy. And it's OK, so don't freak out.

This dad insight has helped me a lot. Since I *do* stress. And I do worry and I do fret. Anyway, I've been doing a lot of self-talk lately. Idk why I think that Jake doesn't like me if he doesn't text me back?

I know—zero logic. So my therapist taught me a cool thing from a famous therapist named Brené Brown: don't make up stories. Meaning don't assume Jake doesn't care for me or doesn't like me, cause I don't get an immediate response.

What if we had to rely solely on snail mail communication? I'd learn to be wayyyy more patient. And stop looking for immediate responses. Sooooo, this is still a work in progress!

My art class is sooooo good! I'm actually a pretty good artist, too. And I'm making good progress. Which has surprised me completely!! My teacher is Ms. Valeria. She's from Colombia originally and has a beautiful accent. She has been an artist since she was young—like 8 years old!! She's taught me so much. I can't believe how much I love this class! I've been pleasantly surprised, that's for sure.

In our first month, we've learned the basics of drawing. Lines. Shading. Shapes. The works. I also have weekly assignments to complete in my sketchbook. It's been challenging, but a good kind of difficult.

I started my classes at our local community college. We call it HCC, and I signed up for just basic general ed classes. They've been pretty chill. Not too easy. Not too difficult. Thankfully, I actually love the campus where all of my classes are held and my professors.

Beth and I have made Tuesday nights our sisters' night. We pick a movie, go to the bookstore, or get a treat. Whatever we do, we just make sure to hang together for a good couple of hours. It's been really great.

I feel like I'm getting to know my sister in a new light. She's really smart—I've always known this—but she's funny and really creative too! She's been working on being more social and not just having her head in a book. In a good way. It's paid off. She's met a cute guy, whose name is Ian, and he's in a few of her classes this year. He's newish to the area, too.

Jake came home once at the end of August. We previously discussed the importance of his spending quality time with Meg and his dad, as they continue to work on their communication. So I see him on Friday nights. And Saturday nights then part of Sunday. This first weekend, when he came home, I was giddy like a kid in a candy store for the first time! Here's how it started:

Jake texts me as he's leaving.

Jake <see you in two and half hours!>

Grace <can't wait!!>

As soon as I read Jake's text and answer, I know I've got two and a half hours before he gets to my house. I make sure I'm dressed nicely and that my hair looks decent.

Then, when I am primped good enough, I head downstairs to check and see that the family room is clean, and decide on an idea for dinner. So that Jake can stay for dinner and then we can watch a movie, I will come up with a few options for us to choose from.

On Friday afternoons, I usually review my assignments due for Monday or complete a project in my art class, and then I can create a plan for my weekend studying. So I make sure to do that too, because before I know it, Jake is HERE.

I run to my front door and greet Jake just as he is about to knock on the door. He scoops me into his arms and we enjoy a passionate kiss! I feel like Jake has been gone for months, and it's literally been two weeks! I know I'm always a little dramatic.

"Oh, I am so glad to SEE YOU, Jake!" I say enthusiastically.

"Me too! It feels like I've been gone forever! And it's only been two weeks!" Jake says, and I laugh as he follows me into our comfy family room.

"I feel the same way, Jake! It feels like it's been soooo long! Come on over and sit by me. I've got a simple dinner for us. Are you feeling up to watching a movie, or would you like to just visit? Beth is at your house tonight, and Mom and Kenneth went out for the evening." I tell Jake.

"I'm down to eat and watch a movie. I'm exhausted!" Jake says.

"I bet you are. I'll get the food. I just picked up some loaded nachos from El Pollo. Let me get them." Jake gives me a thumbs up and settles back onto the couch, and closes his eyes.

I walk into the kitchen and grab a cute serving tray. I load it up with napkins, silverware, the nachos, and two large ice waters. I carefully balance it all and make my way back into the family room. Jake's eyes are still closed. I try to be quiet, but some of the silverware is clinking on one of the glasses.

Jake opens his eyes as he hears the clinking.

"I'm sorry, Jake. If you'd like, we can eat, and then you can head home. I've no problem with this option. Really!" I say smiling, but inside, a pit is forming in my stomach.

Be chill Gracie. Be chill. You'll see him tomorrow night and Sunday afternoon. It's okay . . .

"Nah, I'm okay. Just tired. I'll sleep in tomorrow." Jake grabs a plate and starts loading it with nachos. We alternate between taking bites and talking for a good 20 minutes.

"I feel better. The food pepped me up. What movies did you find for us to watch?" Jake asks me as he adds his plate back onto the tray. I'll deal with it later after Jake goes home.

"Okay, I thought of Shrek, Despicable Me 2, or The Princess Bride," I tell him.

"Oh, The Princess Bride is my choice for sure," he says.

"Cool, let me find it on a platform. Would you mind getting the popcorn containers in the kitchen for us?" I ask him.

"Sure thing." Jake walks to the kitchen, and I pull up the movie. One of our faves.

We settle down on the couch and snuggle close to one another. I click PLAY and the movie starts. Within 20 minutes, I hear soft snores and turn to see that my sweet Jake has fallen asleep!

Poor thing! I'll just clean everything up and then wake him so he can go home.

Ten minutes later, Jake drowsily walks to my front door and outside to his jeep.

"Will you be awake enough to get home okay?" I inquire nervously.

"Yeah, yeah, I'll blast my music," Jake says and leans down to kiss me on my cheek.

"So, like I'll hang with my dad and Meg for a good part of the day and text you later. Are you cool with that?" He asks me.

"Absolutely!" I watch him walk to his Rubicon and get in. His music starts up immediately, and I hear the volume increase. I wave goodbye to him as he pulls out. He waves back, and I see his sweet smile highlighted by the street light on the corner of the street.

Sigh. I'll take any amount of time with that wonderful boy of mine! I think to myself as I close my front door and mosey up the stairs to dream of my beau.

Saturday night, Jake and I thought it would be fun to take our sisters and go miniature golfing together. Kenneth said he'd make homemade pizzas for us all after, and for everyone to give him their choices.

"Jake and Meg? What do you want on your pizzas?" I ask them both.

My boyfriend grins. "As many meats as he can pile on there for me and mushrooms and green peppers, please."

"I'm feeling pineapple and ham personally," Meg adds. I'm texting Kenneth as they tell me.

"Beth?" She looks at me to answer.

"Let's do a margherita for me tonight. So, mozzarella, sauce, and lots of basil."

"Oh, that does sound good. I'll tell Kenneth two of those. My mouth is watering already, and we haven't even started our game!" I laugh, and the other three join me.

"Ditto! Maybe we need a pre-game snack to tide us over until dinner," Beth suggests.

"Yeah, I'm starved too!" Meg chimes in.

We decide to grab some chicken and fries and eat on the way to the miniature golf place. Feeling much better, we get out of the Jeep and head to the course. It's a favorite hang spot with everyone around here, so it's only 5:00 pm, and it's already getting very busy. We all hustle up to the check-in desk, and Jake and I pay for the game. It should take us a good hour and a half, then we'll head to my house for pizza!

We had so much fun together. It was a good idea to take our sisters, Jake and I both decided. Meg really misses Jake. A lot. This is why he will make sure to spend quality time with her and his dad by hanging out together on the Saturdays he's in town.

Sunday night came way too quickly, but we had a great day together, and we all hung out after church. We played games, went for a walk, and ate dinner with my family. Then he was gone. It was really bittersweet to hang with him. I'm working on Tuesdays and Thursdays, but only for a half-day shift after my art class, as I need to balance both my college homework and art projects. Then I work the Saturdays Jake doesn't come into town.

Ha, so I need to interject here and say that I did indeed decide to sign up for the fall semester at class, and apparently, Ms. Valeria—my teacher—has a part two drawing and painting class next semester. I've already signed up! I'm so excited! This semester, we will primarily focus on drawing, and then start painting in the last month of December. Then, get into more painting and mixed media next semester.

15

OCTOBER

By October, our household is in a comfortable routine with Beth, my Mom, and Kenneth. I am also truly enjoying my art class. Who knew I'd actually embrace it and enjoy it? NOT ME that's for sure.

Additionally, a notable development this month is that one of the individuals who runs our local food pantry reached out to me to inquire about volunteering on a weekly basis.

I said yes, and that is what Friday afternoons have been filled with. I am finding out more and more about myself. Between missing Jake, thoughts of my dad, missing Zac, time with Beth, time with Mom and Kenneth, working, going to classes, and taking my art class and therapy once a month.

Between my art class, Tuesday nights with Beth, and food pantry Fridays, I'm discovering who I really am and who I can become. Myself. Not having to depend on my mom, Kenneth, or Jake.

No one but myself. I've made some new friends in some of my college courses as well—super nice girls. I even encouraged one girl, named Heather, to come and volunteer with me on Fridays. She's totally going to do it.

It is Halloween this upcoming Saturday, and Jake will be in town. We're all gathering at my house for a Halloween party! Jake, Meg, his dad, and Samuel. Even Zac and Sarah will be in town, Mom, Kenneth, Beth, and me.

I'm getting "what life was before everyone left" vibes. And I'm super excited.

To say that I miss Jake every day is an understatement. Don't worry. I'll never be like Bella in Book 2 of the Twilight series. Never.

What I am is a girl who loves her boyfriend and misses him, but I'm enjoying this time to really discover what makes me who I am.

I think since my dad died (going on six years now), I've been clinging to his memories and clinging to high school and clinging to what used to be for longer than I realized. Jake leaving has made me realize I have some serious work to do on myself.

Jake is always confident. Like always. Me—not so much. Remember the days when I couldn't believe Jake even paid attention to me or liked me? Yeah. Those days and those feelings and emotions are what I'm tackling now.

My art class, classes, therapy, and volunteer shifts are shaping me. They're showing me what I am capable of doing and also giving me some great ideas for my bachelor's degree, which I've decided will be in public health with an emphasis on non-profit work. In fact, this cute girl in my art class changed seats and came and sat by me.

"Hey, Gracie, is it?" she asks me.

"Yep, and I'm sorry I can't remember what your name is!" I say reddening slightly.

"Michelle. I live near the art house. Do you?" she asks me.

"Yeah, maybe ten minutes away, so not far," I respond to her question.

"I've been wanting to sit by you cause you're a really good artist!" she grins and I just stare at her before answering.

"Well, you're too kind 'cause I just barely think my drawings aren't looking like alien creatures!" I laugh.

"Are you kidding me? You can look at a picture and draw it, and it looks just like it! Sorry, sounds like I'm a creep. I promise I'm not." She laughs as she says this.

"Well, yeah, I'm noticing I'm able to do this. Now, anything from memory is downright awful," I laugh, "but yeah, you're right, I *can* do that. Thanks for noticing, Michelle."

We continue to talk and I find out she's doing the same as I am—minus the long-distance boyfriend—'cause her boyfriend goes to community college, too, lucky duck! She and her boyfriend have classes at the community college. She works, and she found this class sort of like I did, but with a little nudge from her brother, not her mom. We decided to sit by each other in every class from here on out, which makes me super happy.

As I leave class, I continue to ponder what Michelle said to me: I *am* good at looking at pictures and drawing them almost exactly, and I feel happy that I decided to take this class. I am learning a lot about drawing from Ms. Valeria, and I've even been using my drawing assignments as a way to temper any extra emotions I may be feeling. I pop on an audiobook or my Spotify list and draw and draw. It's so therapeutic! It has 100% changed my inner soul. Who knew? Well, I certainly didn't think this would be something I'd enjoy doing. Like ever! My drawing skills always sucked, so I never thought too much about it until my Mom and I were discussing possible creative outlets for me. Just a few weeks ago, if you'd asked me if I'd be enrolled in an art class, I would have said to you, "DREAM ON, and fat chance!"

Art has opened a Pandora's box of amazingness that I never knew existed within me! I've considered myself to be creative, yeah. Sure. But never would I have ever thought of being artistic! Ms. Valeria is absolutely incredible.

She's encouraging. She's kind. But she's honest and offers helpful criticism so we can improve and understand how to draw things. It's been delightful. Anyway, another tangent, but how could I know that this would all happen this semester?

I didn't have a clue that staying home would turn out to be incredible instead of awful. Gotta go. It's Tuesday, and Beth and I are finishing up our awesome Halloween costumes. Three more days until Jake is home!

❄

Jake <GRACIE ON THE WAY TO YOU>

Gracie <ohhhhh yeahhhhh can't wait to see you>

Jake <ditto>

Gracie <Beth, and I got our costumes already. Are you and Meg ready>

Jake <thankfully Meg has handled this for us. Phew>

Gracie <see you soon at my house Kenneth is making the home-made pizza deliciousness meal>

Jake <dude can't wait bye xoxo>

Gracie <xoxo>

I sigh a happy sigh. And yeah. You saw what you saw. We've been putting X's and O's to end our texts. So many heart-eyes emojis fill my heart. It's around 2 pm. I'm cleaning the house with Mom, Beth, Kenneth, and Meg.

We need to set up the kitchen for dinner first. Then, we've got the dining room table covered with all the Halloween paraphernalia for tomorrow night's festivities.

The Halloween party is great: small and simple, but it's a nice time together as a family. After, Jake asks me if I want to walk to the park and talk for a bit.

I didn't see him during the day on Saturday—that's his family day—so since we always have limited time when we can be together, we make the most of it. We usually go out or hang out on Friday and Saturday nights, then part of Sunday.

"Hey, Mom, Jake and I are gonna go take a walk for a bit before everybody leaves. OK?" I ask my mom.

"Sure. If you guys can just be home by 11:30 pm, that would be great." She tells me as she glances at her watch. I glance at mine. 10:35 pm.

"Uh, yeah. That should be no problemo. Bye!"

Jake is waiting by the front door. He and Meg dressed up as Winnie the Pooh characters, Jake as Pooh, Meg as Tigger, and their dad as Eeyore. Jake looks adorable in anything. For realz. Beth, Mom, Kenneth, and I dressed up as Smurfs. Kenneth is Smurfette, Mom is Papa Smurf, I am Brainy Smurf, and Beth is Vanity Smurf.

And no, I did not paint myself blue. None of us did. We just found some cute costumes and went with that. Zac and Sarah dressed up as the Incredibles couple.

I smile as I come towards Jake and the already open front door. He gently takes my hand and we walk out into the cooler air. October has been kind to us. The heat has subsided. And temperatures are in the 70s.

Thank goodness. We take our time walking to the park. We're both sort of quiet. I think that when we come together like this, it takes us a bit to acclimate to each other. I think there are a lot of feelings in both of us. I am glad to know that he misses me as much as I miss him. He has been working so hard in his classes.

He took a pretty good load for his first semester. And will do the same for the second semester. As we walk hand-in-hand to the swings, my mind jumps back to one of the first times we did this together and then the many, many times we have continued to walk to our little park to talk, to visit, to be with each other, and just swing on the swings together. This night is no different. But there has been a great amount of growth and maturity for both of us.

"Jake, how are you really holding up at school? Are you feeling like you're able to do your classes? Are your roommates good? Do you feel like you're getting enough food?" I ask him as we slowly swing back and forth. A gentle breeze blows to his dark hair and sweeps it off his forehead as he looks at me with his amazing, beautiful, kind, blue eyes.

"You know, it's hard to be away from you, Meg, and my dad, more than I realized. Now, don't get me wrong. I can handle it. I love my roommates. And it's kind of cool because we all have girlfriends, and Robert and I both have girlfriends back home. So it's kind of cool to have someone I can talk to about it. My classes are great. I love studying business. I just keep pushing forward. Thankfully, for my Econ class and my stats class, there are labs and tutors available to help. So I go in there. And that's helpful. I try to study at the library every day."

He continues. "I eat my meals in the cafeteria, and Robert and I hang out a lot, which has made it great. We even have a few classes together. He's also studying business. And Sam and Conner knew each other before they got into this apartment, and they're both going into Finance."

Jake pauses, then adds. "Sometimes I feel really lonely. I'm not gonna lie. I'm sure you feel the same way. Sometimes I wish I could just pick you up and we could go for a drive. We could go out to eat. We could do any of the things that we used to do together. But I'm OK. And I feel like we're both growing and maturing right now. Would you agree?"

"Absolutely. I had no idea that I would love my art class. I could never have predicted that I would even be in one. I am volunteering on Fridays. And I love it. More than I had anticipated. And I really, really like working in a nonprofit. Our volunteer work was a great experience. But it was the four of us, and we all went in together, so I like this volunteer work because it is different. This is me. This is Gracie learning new things. I'm going to get trained on the intake process next month. Super excited about that. And I love my classes."

He smiles at me, and it gives me encouragement to continue.

"I've a couple of friends that I've met too. One girl named Michelle, I think I've told you about in art class. And most of all, Beth and I have become much better sisters and friends together. Beth has a cute guy that she really likes. But she's not worried about you hanging out with him, but he's come around a few times. She's such a bookworm; she's trying to expand herself socially. That's why we do things together every Tuesday night. I'm helping her to come out of her shell a bit more this week. So yeah, I feel the same way. I miss you every day. I wish we could do the same thing. We could go and eat. We could go to a movie. We could just walk together, just like we are right now. And hang out at the park. And talk together, but I think it's been good for us to see how we are as individuals without being together every minute of every day. Would I change it? I probably would. But maybe a part of me, because I wouldn't have thought that Beth and I would be hanging out more. Or that I would be doing these other things that I mentioned."

"I agree with you there, Gracie. If I could change it, I would, and I wouldn't. Some days it's super hard. Some days it's not as hard. I never thought that I'd have a girlfriend whom I would miss every day. He laughs. "But I love to hear about the amazing things that you're involved in. I love to hear about you and Beth hanging out together. I love to hear about your mom and her success and tennis and how much she loves your mom and that your mom loves him."

"Yeah, well, this girl here never thought she'd have a boyfriend. And one as amazing as you. And one who's so good to his sister and so good to his dad. The one who keeps the family together, despite having his mom gone. I admire how strong you've been," I reply.

Jake blushes a little. "Yes... well..."

"I mean it," I say. "I'm also glad that you're able to concentrate on your studies even when you travel back and forth home on some weekends, without being too terribly sad and heartbroken. I'm also glad that you're still getting along well with your mom. I am so happy to hear about her and her success. And she is moving forward with it. And has a job. And has gotten into pottery. I didn't even know that she did Art either. But maybe she can figure out what she wants to be in her life. And why doesn't she feel fulfilled?!"

"Yeah. Her friend says that she also makes pottery, also, and they're going to start selling it at an outdoor open market. I'm glad for my mom. I will never agree with how she has done everything. But I'm happy for her. Do I wish it were different? I do. My dad is pretty lonely. Thankfully, he can travel here and there, and he has a great team to work with. But of course, that leaves me behind. But there lies another thing I'm most happy and grateful for: you and your family. I don't even know what I would do without you guys," Jake says more softly.

I know it hurts his heart to have his mom gone. I know it hurts his heart to have a sister miss him and be lonely. Jake is at school, and his dad is traveling. But I also know that he is grateful for our family. And my family adores Meg.

She is a ray of sunshine in our home. And she has been doing a lot of work on herself and figuring out how she feels about her mom being gone, with my therapist. So for that, I'm super happy for her. Beth and Meg have a great rapport, which makes me feel very happy.

Jake slows his swing, and I do the same. He gets off and comes towards me, pulling me into him in his warm and comforting embrace. We linger in this embrace for a good 10 minutes. He kisses the top of my head, and he tells me that he misses me a lot.

But he's grateful that they are able to spend weekends together. I tell him I agree and that I'm thankful we can do this, because I know it doesn't work out for all people to see each other as often as we do.

Breaking away from each other, I take his hand in mine, and we quietly walk back to the house—another beautiful time and evening spent with an amazing human.

16

NOVEMBER

"How can it be November already?" Beth says with somewhat of an aggravated tone.

"I agree, Beth, I feel like the semester is flying by. I don't know if that's good or bad?" I respond to her.

"For real. I'm not sure if I think it's a good or a bad thing. Maybe it just is. Nonetheless, Thanksgiving will be here before we know it. What is Jake doing with his family? Have you talked to him? Because Meg is saying that they are going to go on a family trip together," Beth tells me.

"Yeah, that's a suck fest. I really wanted to spend the whole week with Jake, but it's okay, I'm sure I'll get through this. I'm sure he will, too. And I'm sure they need some family time together. We can't always be together, all of us, or can we?" I say with a laugh.

"Yeah, I'm not quite sure you two can handle a full week without each other when you know you could be spending that time together," Beth teases.

"Oh, you're so funny!" I chuckle.

"If we can handle three months without each other, then I feel we can handle a week without each other. I will just focus on Christmastime when we will have three weeks together." I smile happily.

"Yeah, I mean, I'm not gonna have my Bestie with me either. But I think I'll be OK," Beth replies. "Plus, Zach will be home all week with us. Did you hear that Sarah is taking a trip with her family? Actually, this might be a stellar time for us to catch up and hang out together again, just like we used to in the old days."

"Oh my gosh. You're totally right. We can have game day Sundays, two of them, or rather play games all week. We could go to the movies together. We can just watch movies here together. I think that's gonna be pretty awesome. Thank you for reminding me of that —that helps me not to feel as sad," I tell Beth.

Before I know it, it's the week of Thanksgiving. Jake didn't even get to come home from Austin; instead, his dad and Meg drove to Austin, and then they flew back to Austin after their trip. They decided to spend a week in Florida and spend time together on the beach. Of course, I'm completely jealous, because I love the beach, but I am also extremely happy for them all. It's not like we can't text, call, or FaceTime every day.

Zac came home on Sunday, the week before Thanksgiving. Sarah left early Monday morning. And we three are having the most fun together we've had in a long time. We can just be together and laugh together about nothing.

We all love it so much. We talk about our futures together. Zac tells us many funny stories, as a pre-med student, about his classes and his labs. Beth even shares about the guy she likes, whose name is Ian. I didn't know she'd ever tell Zac that! And that he was going to come and take her out this weekend. Zach and I look at each other. I knew we had to delve into that conversation immediately.

"Who said our little sister could go out with anybody?" I say to Beth.

"Uh, yeah. That can't be happening, can it? Right before our eyes, Gracie?" Zac responds, smiling.

"Okay, so you two need to settle down! Sheesh. We're just friends. And his name is Ian. Although he's a very hot friend, I doubt he thinks of me as anything more than just friends." Beth sighs, rolling her eyes.

"Okay wait. Are you kidding me? If he's asking you out, he's already into you," Zac says. "I know. I'm a guy. I know how we think."

"It's true. That's how Jake and I started. Friends. Good friends. I like that way, way better than a first date and kissing right out of the gate, all in the beginning, while you're just trying to get to know each other. That's def not for me, and no way would Zac and I ever let you do that, little sister!" Zac and I burst out laughing. Beth just glares at us with a smirk.

"Will you two RELAX already? We're hanging out, not going on a date; there's a big difference." Beth says matter-of-factly.

"Okay, we'll relax, but do we get to MEET this boy you will be hanging out with this weekend?" I ask.

"Yeah, will we?" Zac chimes in.

"Of course, you two don't let me do anything unless it passes your approval." Beth frowns, but her tone is light.

"So tell us about this Ian guy, Beth," I say.

"For real, spill!" Zac adds.

"He's just in a few of my classes, okay, no big deal. He's nice and smart and doesn't make fun of me answering questions and getting the highest grades, so that alone makes him a winner in my book of life!" Beth states.

"Oh yeah, that IS good. No one needs to be mocked for being themselves! Hate that so much for you, Beth." I mutter.

"Sorry, Beth," Zac says softly.

"Okay! Let's play Racko and break up these nonsensical feelings! I'm good." Beth leaps up from her seated position on the floor, grabs Racko off the game shelf, and heads for the dining room table. "Let's go, you two!"

"Okay, okay, we're coming!" I yell back. I walk into the dining room with Zac right behind me. We both join Beth at the table and begin to play Racko.

Thanksgiving week came and went. We met Ian, and as Beth had told us, he was indeed a great kid. Zac and I gave Beth a thumbs up to Ian, and we figured we'd definitely be seeing more of Ian at our house, too.

Sarah came back late Sunday night. She and Zac headed out for college that next Monday morning. Not seeing Jake all week was rough, but I made it through! You'd be proud of me! I texted Jake sporadically.

I kept my emotions to myself and let myself enjoy my siblings. Was it easy? HECK NO. It was hard. I didn't know when Jake and I started hanging out together that I'd like him this much or that I'd miss him as much as I do.

Not that I've ever really dated anyone, except for hanging out with guy and girl friends over the years. So, you know, new territory. New emotions. Basically, a lot of new things.

17

———————

DECEMBER

December is here, and with it comes finals before school lets us all out just before Christmas. Jake will be home on December 23rd. Zac is going to travel with Sarah and her family on a European trip.

I'm not jelly AT ALL. J/k, I really am! I told Zac he HAD to bring me at least a few souvenirs so I could pretend I'd been to Europe.

Brooke and Justin will be home too! We four plan to hang out as much as possible with each other. I'm taking work off too. I have a lot of art projects to do before the end of my class. I have worked really hard on my drawing.

Like I practice every night, which is one thing I did over Thanksgiving break that helped a lot in pushing down any excess emotions I tried to conjure up.

Ms. Valeria is so good at teaching us how to draw! My class is small. About seven of us, so Ms. Valeria can come around and take the necessary time to help us on an individual level.

It's been so good for me. I'll send pics of my drawings to Jake, and he's been very impressed! I'm impressed with myself, too! Just the other day, Ms. Valeria sat down next to me and helped with my shading. It's the hardest skill for me to get! Sheesh, Idk why.

"Gracie, wow! That apple looks very realistic. I love the contour here (she points to the left of my apple drawing) and the shading is coming along well," she tells me.

"Are you sure? I think the way I'm shading looks so weird to me!" I laugh.

"Yep, I've seen you greatly improve this semester. So let me show you one thing I do if I get stuck." Ms. Valeria grabs a tiny flashlight and shines it on the real apple in the middle of our table, which we're using as our still life to learn to shade.

"See that?" She points out the shadow and where it lands. "Even if I've shown you this a few times, it's good to use this technique until your brain can envision where the shading should be." She tells me in her beautiful, thick accent.

"Okay! I will practice this at home. That really does help me! Thank you, Ms. Valeria," I say to her with a relieved smile. Tbh, the shading part of drawing this still life assignment is REALLY stressing me out! I'm sure she could see it on my face!

I continue to work on the shading part until it's time to go. I love that this class is two hours, too. It gives me a good amount of time to listen, learn, and then try to reproduce what Ms. Valeria has taught us. I finish up for the day, pack up, and head to my car. I planned my Tuesdays and I have been working Thursdays since August so that I could always go home, get lunch, pack snacks, and change clothes before starting my shift at Sicily's. I'm grateful to have a few shifts per week. Gives me some different types of socialization while earning money.

I am so grateful to be able to be at home for the next two years and continue to build my savings while I can. Saving my money helps me feel excited about reapplying to UT Austin next year. I don't know if it was fate or whatever that I didn't get into UT Austin, but even though I miss Jake, I've had some thoroughly great experiences with Beth and in my art class, college classes, and volunteering on Fridays.

These four things have been extremely worthwhile. Who knows if these experiences are meant to add to my personality and skill set? But it certainly feels like they're making me a better ME.

I have a great shift today and head home to start planning my study schedule for finals week. Next week will be a beatdown for sure.

And then, in one week, Jake is home, and Brooke, Justin, Meg, Beth, and I are all out of high school and college! I can hardly wait. Have I mentioned that before? 'Cause I am STOKED!

And it's here! Finals week has arrived! Jake is crazy busy, as am I; Beth and Meg are studying every single day, as am I! It's the worst week of the year, and we always have two of them! But, I can handle anything this week, knowing that Friday is fast approaching.

Two great things will happen this Friday: I will volunteer, and I am now trained on the intake process (checking people in, their names, family members, and what food they can get, depending on that information). ALSO, Jake will be home! Back to studying! I have a lot to study, and I will finish my first semester drawing course this Thursday, so I am slammed, which is a great way to distract me from counting down the days until FRIDAY!

AND I MADE it to Friday morning also, idk if I mentioned, it's also three days before Christmas is HERE, and I have one more final this morning, then I'll go and volunteer. So far, all of my finals have gone pretty darn good, if I do say so myself!

And my art class ended so wonderfully yesterday! Sigh. Ms. Valeria is magical and I soooo look forward to taking part two starting at the end of January. But, I need to get home! I'm dawdling like crazy cause my brain is so full of, well, everything good!

My final is at 10 am this morning, so I'm in good shape time-wise, but I still am taking a little too much time on getting ready. However, I do need to look really nice when Jake comes home tonight. I am wearing my fave flared jeans, my Docs, and a soft peachy colored shorty sweatshirt, with a cute tee underneath.

I am taking my time on my makeup and my hair, too. Hey! I want to look very kissable. Huggable? Ha, both.

In route to my volunteer shift, I think of how glad I am to be finally done with all of my finals. Argh, it takes a lot to get good grades and study for these courses. I muse over these thoughts, humming to my excellent playlist, and arrive ten minutes before my shift.

I try not to look too gussied up so as not to make anyone feel uncomfortable while I am helping them to get their food, so I changed to a black sweatshirt and my black Hokas (I know these are expensive, but I have to wear them on the blasted cement floor) and put my hair into a ponytail. I usually wear my small silver hoop earrings too, and no other jewelry. Oh, but I always wear the necklace Jake gave me.

I just tuck it down into any shirt I'm wearing. I put in the door code to the side door that leads into the donations unloading area and check in with my boss, Dennis.

"Hey, hey, how's it going, Gracie?" Dennis addresses me as I enter his office.

"Hey, Dennis, really good 'cause my finals are donezo!" I grin ear to ear.

"Ah, finals. Ha. Don't miss those days! Anyway," Dennis begins. "Let's get you on the intake shift. How did you feel about it last week? Sorry, I wasn't here to follow up with you, but I heard from Kara and she said you did fabulously, which doesn't surprise me one bit." Dennis gives me a warm smile that makes his eyes wrinkle and twinkle. It's so sweet.

"Well, all the credit goes to Kara because she trained me! I did feel okay about everything. There were a few mistakes I made here and there, but Kara was right by my side to help me. Is she helping me again today?" I ask earnestly.

"Yes, this week and then after New Year's, she will help you two more times if you think you need it," Dennis tells me.

"Okay, cool, cool. I'm ready to go. Let me put up my purse and find Kara. Thanks, Dennis!"

My shift flew by! Wow! My shift is 2 1/2 hours. Once started today, it was a madhouse. I helped 45 people get food, which was about eight families. Many of them are already in the system. Some were new clients today.

So if they're new, I have a few things to do to enter their information in, get their ID, and get the details on their family dynamics. But I did better than last week. I'm getting the hang of it, so that makes me feel better. I can't believe how many people needed food today. Really put a lot of thought into my mind.

Thoughts about other people. Thoughts about those who don't have anywhere near what I have every day. I never have to worry about a meal. I never have to worry about a bed. I never have to worry about shelter. I think that the shift as a volunteer for the local Food.

Pantry is something that is going to be life-changing for me. Because I can feel my soul and my thinking change rapidly. I felt very humble today. I also felt very, very grateful for all that I have.

I hear my phone get a text message. I'm almost home, so I'm being a good driver and will wait until I'm home to read my text. I pull the car into the driveway, put it in park, and grab my cell.

Yassssssssssssssssssss

Jake just texted me to say that he will leave by 5 pm, which is in a few hours. I am so happy because I'm done with art class, with college classes, and work. I will spend the next two weeks enjoying my family, friends, and my adorable boyfriend. Who wouldn't be happy?

Jake <guess who's on his way back to you>

Gracie <OH my gosh I'm soooo happy>

Jake <me too time together sleeping in and no classes!>

Gracie <amen to that, I'm done with everything too! Three weeks of relaxation, here we come>

Jake <I'll be at your house probs by 8 pm and I'll swing by cool>

Gracie <fab see you then be safe >

I love that our texting is short and sweet, but effective. Okay, I've got two full hours, I will do a quick pick up of the family room, eat some dinner, and then read my book that I haven't picked up for a few weeks until Jake gets here.

Mom and Kenneth have gone out for the night, but Beth and Meg will be here tonight with Jake and me. At my house, we've been watching Christmas movies since Thanksgiving, and we are continuing the fun tonight with *A Christmas Story*. We are looking forward to watching this movie. It is one of my faves.

I hear a knock at the door, and then I hear Jake open it and walk in. "Gracie?"

I basically sprint from the family room to the front entry area.

"Oh my gosh, you're here!" I throw my arms around his neck and meet his lips with mine. It is beyond good to be in Jake's arms and to be kissing him again. It's been a long almost two months, that's for sure.

We engage in a nice, long, and tender kiss. Then break apart to walk into the family room hand in hand (I changed back into my cutie outfit, put down my hair, curled it, and pulled my necklace out of my sweatshirt. Girls gotta look fresh). Beth and Meg are already on the couch, movie teed up. Meg jumps up and hugs her brother.

"Missed you, bro," Meg says sweetly.

"You too, sis. You too." Jake responds tenderly. Meg returns to her spot, Jake and I, and we join her on the couch. I already popped us some popcorn and made us all hot chocolate.

Poor Jake fell asleep about halfway through. He is so tired from the semester and the drive. I snuggle in close to him and the girls, and I finish the movie. I wake Jake up, and he and Meg head home. We all four plan to meet up later tomorrow after a long sleep-in.

We will need to do some last-minute Christmas shopping to finish up our gift buying before Christmas. I previously asked for some ideas from Meg and Mr. Hansen, Jake's dad, on what to get Jake for Christmas. I just need to get Jake one more thing, and then I'm done!

Phew! Thank goodness. I was stressing out about this big time. I bought him a few things, but I still need a few more gifts for him. I also need to get a few more things for Beth, since I'm in charge of her gifts. We have a great family tradition where we each draw a name every year to see who each person will buy for, then Mom and dad, well Kenneth now, supply us each with $250 to get gifts for the person they are to shop for. This year, it's just Mom, Kenneth, Beth, and me. It's been a great tradition and we really end up making Christmas about being together more than the gifts. We started this when all of us were very young!

I sleep until about 11:30 AM. Boy, does it feel amazing. The semester has been wonderful, but you know how a semester can be.

Very long, stressful, and busy. So, having finals done, having my volunteer work paused until after Christmas, and having my art class done are all awesome.

I grab my phone and check for texts.

Jake <morning sleepy head! As soon as you wake up, text me!>

Brooke <hey Justin and I will come in tomorrow to the Austin airport. Let's make plans for the day after Christmas, okay?>

Mom <breakfast is on the counter>

Beth <get up and get dressed, let's go!>

I quickly respond to everyone. Make my bed. Think of what to wear as I shower. Weather-wise, it's in the 60s, which is code for jeans and a coat. I throw on one of my new sweaters I bought recently, grab my face jeans from the floor, and lace up my Hokas.

I put my hair into a ponytail and apply simple makeup, but put on my lip stain. I grab my crossbody purse and coat and head out of my room and downstairs to eat. Jake and Meg will be at our house in ten minutes. I scarf down my scrambled eggs and two muffins. I wash it all down with a delicious glass of very cold vitamin D milk. Mmmmmm

"Thanks for saving me breakfast, Mom!" I yell to her through the office door. She and Kenneth are wrapping gifts in mom's and I guess now Kenneth's office (I always call it mom's though, cause you know it was hers first).

"You're welcome, sweetie!" Mom yells back at me.

"I'll text you when we get to the mall and tell you what we're doing, okay?"

"Sure, sure. Have fun!" Mom tells me.

"Bye, Kenneth. Have fun wrapping you two!" I say loudly. I'm standing by the door now.

"Bringing me pure Christmas joy that's for sure!" Kenneth says happily, but with obvious sass.

I laugh and call up to Beth.

"To Beth let's go! Now I'm waiting on you?" I laugh.

Beth hustles down the stairs—purse and coat in her arms.

"Please. I've been up for hours. How do you sleep for so long?" She grins at me.

"Uh, how is it that you don't sleep in longer?" I retort.

"Pfffd. I don't know. I just like to get up and get stuff done," Beth says.

"Yeah yeah, I know. Miss Efficient." I snort. "Let's go. Jake and Meg are here!"

I'm sooo happy Jake is home. I can't even express in words how I feel. I feel super happy and comfortable, like putting on your favorite cozy sweatshirt, or like opening a gift you've really wanted. You feel true happiness! That's sort of how I'm feeling right now.

I'm smiling as I walk out our door. Beth locks it behind us and we hop into the Rubicon (it's pumped up so even at 5'6" and 5'8" we have to jump up a bit).

"Hey you! Feels good to see you in real life!" I smile and lean over to kiss him.

He kisses me back. I close my eyes and revel in the moment.

We break apart and Jake grabs my hand.

"Oh, how I've missed you!" He says to me and squeezes my hand, and smiles his beautiful smile at me.

Sighhhhh. Like my fave cozy sweatshirt. Safe. Comfortable. Happy.

"Oh, goody. The lovebirds are back together again," Meg grins. She and Beth burst into laughter.

"Just you wait, Meg. You'll find someone you adore one day. Just you wait, and then I can tease you right back!" I turn and tell her, smiling.

"Oh, she DOES have someone she likes!" Beth blurts out.

"Umm excuse me?" Jake says, sounding very brotherly and protective, as he looks at Meg in his rearview window.

"Beth! Shut it!" But Meg is laughing and blushing.

"His name is Alex. And guess what? Alex is Ian's best friend. How cool is that?" Beth shares.

"Wait, that's actually very cool. Love that. So are we going to see Ian and Alex this Christmas break then?" I ask them both.

"Yes!" Beth says, blushing.

"Okay, then let's plan a game night or something with all six of us.

Is that cool with you girls? Will Ian and Alex be cool with that? I guess I should ask?" I say to both Beth and Meg.

"Let me see what they're doing for the break. We will let you two know," Beth answers me.

The rest of the drive to the mall, Jake and I fall into comfortable conversation, mostly about how our little sisters are not little anymore. Beth and Meg are fully engrossed in talking about Ian and Alex. It's cute to see that they both seem to have nice guys they like.

We pull into the parking lot. It's packed.

"Ugh. Welcome to Christmas at the mall!" I say.

"Okay, let's just get this over with so we can go and hang out together," Jake tells me.

"Agreed," I respond to him. "Let's go, girls."

We jump down from the Rubicon, put on our coats, and walk as a group toward the mall entrance. We stop and make a shopping plan.

"Okay, I've got three places I need to go to," I say.

"K. I've got four," Jake chimes in after me.

"We have five. But I need to go with you, Gracie, for the gifts I need," Beth tells me as she looks at me.

"Okay, so let's switch up and meet back in what two hours and eat something at the food court? Or should we leave and get something to eat somewhere else?" Jake says to all of us.

"Definitely somewhere else," Meg replies with finality.

"Okay. Decision made then," he laughs. "Okay. Let's get this done." Jake leans over and kisses me on the cheek.

"Have fun, girls!" He says to Beth and me.

"Bye! You guys have fun too," I call back.

"Let's go!" I grab Beth by her arm and we get moving. We've got to hit the bookstore, various clothing stores, and the Lego store. It takes us the entire two hours to get everything we want to buy. Same with Jake and Meg.

Jake texts me and suggests just meeting at his Rubicon. Too crazy in the mall!

Jake <you girls done? Can you meet at my car?>

Gracie <totally. Beth is finishing her last purchase. Meet you guys

there. Ten minutes>

Jake <perf thx>

Luckily, Jake's Rubicon is big cause we all had a lot of packages. We load the packages into the back of the jeep, trying to squeeze everything in without breaking anything. Dang. We bought a lot today!

Loaded up. Seat belts buckled. Christmas tunes on, we cruise carefully through the very overcrowded parking lot. Jake is a great driver. Thankfully. He's not ever risky. Grateful for that.

"Where should we eat, guys?" I ask the three of them.

"What if we order some wings and fries and head back home?" Meg suggests.

"Oh yes. Good idea!" Beth agrees. "I'm starving!"

Jake calls in the order. I shoot a text to mom to see if she and Kenneth will be around.

Gracie <hey mom we want to order wings and fries for all of us. You guys are going to be home>

Mom <yummo, yes please, and pay for it using the family debit card, please>

Gracie <will do thanks, see you soon>

Mom <*thumbs up*>

"All good, and mom and Kenneth will pay for it all, so sweet!" I say to all of them.

"That is so nice of them. I'm starved too!" Jake responds enthusiastically.

Wings and fries retrieved, we head home.

Everyone is starving, so the plan for the night is to eat, then watch a movie, then head home early. Every one of us has a lot of wrapping to do before Monday, and tomorrow evening is Christmas Eve. We're having Samuel, Jake, and Meg, of course. Zac and Sarah will Face-Time us on Christmas Day since they're in the Bahamas. Lucky for them! Sheesh. I want to go to the beach! But, hey, let's be real! No need for me to be jelly, right? Right! I've got the rest of my family, my boyfriend, and his family here in town, so I'm good.

Dinner complete- check

Movie- check

Dead tired from a great day-check

Boy, am I glad to FINALLY be in my bed. This was a very busy, but both productive and fun Saturday. I'm so tired I can't even muster enough energy to read on my Kindle. I need sleep. Thankfully, tomorrow, we just have one hour of church at 10 am, then we're chilling at our own houses until about 4 pm. This will be my third Christmas with Jake. Well, we just started hanging out that first Christmas, so I guess it's really our second one together.

I am on cloud 50, having more than a day and a half to hang with Jake, finally! I think I've been doing just fine with him being gone and only seeing him twice a month, but now that he's been here for nearly three weeks, I am so very happy.

He's so kind, so beautiful, so thoughtful, so smart, and the list goes on. My goal is to soak in every minute with him. I need to gear up for the freaking second semester! I'll be fine, but man oh man, I love being with this amazing boy!

I sit on my bed and grab my journal, which is always in my side table drawer. It's almost filled up already! That's crazytown. I start writing.

I try to write out my feelings, but I don't even have enough words to express how it feels to have Jake here in real time by my side again. I missed him dearly. I definitely consider him my best friend. I'm about to lie down and snuggle in for the night when I hear my phone vibrate. It's nearly midnight.

Jake <Gracie I had such a good time with you last night and today. I don't think I realized how much I miss being physically with you, ya know, until I've been gone so much and now can be with you every day again. It's good to be home, it's even better to be with you>

Gracie <my journal just got an earful about all of those same things. I am so happy you're here, so very happy. Sleep well>

Jake <you too>

With Jake's sweet words whirling around in my mind, I lie my tired, but ecstatic self down onto my pillow and happily drift off to sleep.

18

JANUARY (SECOND SEMESTER OF COLLEGE)

"Bye! Jake! See you in two weeks!" I yell as Jake puts his Rubicon into reverse to pull out of my driveway.

I'm hating this deja vu moment so freaking much! My heart actually hurts. I don't want Jake to leave! I hate saying goodbye. HATE IT!

I keep a pasted smile on my face as I continue to wave goodbye until I can't see Jake anymore.

I'm not gonna cry, I'm not gonna cry!

Hoping that my self-talk will somehow magically halt the tears, but, unfortunately, I feel them prick my eyes and warm my cheeks as they fall like dripping raindrops on the windowpane. Ugh. STOP.

I don't want to talk to anyone, so I quietly enter our house and silently creep upstairs to my room. I feel like I'm in a drama right now as I throw myself on my bed onto my stomach. I allow myself to cry for no more than ten minutes, then I force myself up off my bed, check my face in my mirror, snatch my art bag off the floor, and seat myself at my desk.

I put in my AirPods, cranked up Charli XCX, and started to draw and draw. Flowers. Faces. Trees. Anything I can think of to draw, I do so. Next, I pull out my first semester portfolio and review it, looking for some other ideas to draw. I see a sun with a face.

We worked on drawing suns with different faces briefly in November. I remember now that I really liked it, so I grab my sketch book and find a large jar and trace around it to make a nice, round circle.

I scroll on my phone to my Pinterest app and type in "sun faces," and so many pop up. I quickly make a new folder and pin a whole bunch of faces into the folder. I know it takes almost three hours for Jake to get to UT Austin, so I plan to flood my brain with tunes and draw until I feel less agitated.

Two hours later, I look over my drawings.

Oh my! I love drawing suns. I love making different designs and colors on them! And, most of all, I feel good. I feel okay. I don't feel sad, I feel satisfied, I guess I'd say, not overwhelmed by a mountain of sad, lonely feelings trying to squish me. Good, good.

It's nearly 8:00 pm when I waltz downstairs to see what's happening with my family. I hear laughter from the dining room and head that way.

"Hey everyone. And before you say anything, I'm good," I say abruptly.

Mom gets up from her chair and gives me a tender hug. She speaks softly into my ear. "I came to check on you and saw you listening to music and drawing, so I let you be. I'm super proud of you for using that as a coping technique. I know this separation from Jake is so yuck, and I'm sorry." She kisses my cheek, takes my hand, and leads me to the table. It looks as if the three of them had just finished a game of Racko.

"Join us, sweetie," Kenneth says to me, and starts gathering up the cards. He shuffles them and deals them out among the four of us.

I give everyone a weak smile and sit down. Another two hours fly by before I know it. We had the best time playing both Racko and UNO.

"Night, everyone, and thanks." I smile for real now and head upstairs to bed, but as I turn to go, I feel Beth take my arm and walk with me up to my room.

"You good, Gracie?" Beth asks me.

I sit on the edge of my bed and face her. She's sitting on my desk chair.

"You know, Beth, I can say yes, I do to that question and with real conviction. I cranked my tunes, and I drew and drew. It was good. I am still surprised how much it helped me not to focus all my feels on Jake being gone—again. He even texted me when we were playing games, but I didn't answer and kept playing. So, now I will answer him. What do you think about that?" I say smiling.

"I say that's incredible progress, and I'm really proud of you! Look at you go, girl, I mean like what?" Beth praises me.

"Thanks, Beth. Good luck starting your new semester tomorrow, by the way." I smile.

"Thanks. I'm ready. I can only take sooo much time off from school, you know that." She laughs.

"Amen to that! I start in one week, but art starts this week, so yay for that," I tell her.

"Good! You are getting really good. Keep it up!" Beth says and hugs me as she heads out of my room.

I pick up my phone and read the text from Jake.

Jake <made it safely, missed you the moment I left>

Gracie <ditto to that, I did some drawing and the four of us played games>

Jake <sorry I had to go back early, but in order to get a summer internship, I had to get back early. I have to apply, so this week I'm writing my essay and filling out the application. Robert is back early, too; he's trying to get an internship like me. It's so competitive. Bleh.>

Gracie <I'm so glad Robert is there with you. What about the other guys?>

Jake <they'll be back on Friday>

Gracie <kk glad you're safe, sleep well>

Jake <you too see you in two weeks>

Gracie <*heart*>

I quickly wash my face, brush my hair and my teeth, and crawl in between my sheets, pulling my comforter close to my chin.

I grab my wooby (my soft, little blankie I put over my eyes to help me sleep), pick up my Kindle, find my bookmarked spot, and pick up where I left off last night, distracting myself from missing Jake, which does actually help. I begin to nod off, so I place my Kindle back on my side table and close my weary eyes.

Here's hoping my dreams are sweet, not sour.

THE WEEK PASSES QUICKLY, THANKFULLY. JAKE WON'T BE HOME UNTIL the weekend after this upcoming one. I'm okay with that. We've been able to text a lot more since neither of us has started school yet.

I do get to volunteer today at the food pantry. Three weeks is a long time off, so I sure hope I remember how to do everything! I arrive ten minutes early as recommended and check in with Kara.

"Hello! How was your Christmas and New Year's break?" I ask Kara.

"Hi, Grace! It was wonderful. My husband's family came into town for a week, and my kids adore them," Kara shares with me.

"Aww that's so great! Good to hear. Okay, I'm ready to do the intake again. Hoping I remember everything," I say.

"Oh, you will. You've got this down. No problem. And you know if you need help, I'm here for you!" Kara reassures me.

I smile and walk over to the intake table.

One thing I need to ask Kara or Dennis is, what the heck do people do when the pantry is closed over the holidays? These thoughts have been on my mind for a while now, especially with all the stuff we got for Christmas and the activities we did together. We spent a lot of money. That's for sure.

I open the Google tab for the intake sheet. I've got three people sitting in the waiting area, and a sweet older lady approaches the table.

"Hello, my name is Grace. How can I help you today?"

"Oh, hello, Grace. I've never been here before. What do I need to do to get some food? My husband just died and left me with medical bills. My Social Security barely covers all of my bills for the month,"

The sweet lady says. I can see tears starting to well up in her eyes, so I reach across the table and pat her hand.

"First of all, I need your ID, please, so I can enter your personal info."

This sweet lady's name is Anna Maria Gonzalez. She's from Mexico City and has been here in Texas for 15 years. I type everything in. I ask her more questions and then ask if there are others in the household. It's just her now. I feel so sad for her.

Once I've got all the info I need, I can now give her the list of items she can get. The pantry recently got an overhaul, and now it looks like a grocery store. On the list of items, whoever does the intake will circle what the client is eligible for.

The eligibility is based on the number of people per household. I fill out the sheet for Anna Maria and then tell her I am going to send her over to another volunteer who will show her how to fill up the rolly cart. I give her a laminated sheet with the items she's eligible to choose.

Since I am now volunteering at the front check-in desk doing data entry per client, I no longer work in the grocery store area, so I pass her off to another volunteer, say goodbye, then turn back to the laptop and continue checking in the other waiting clients.

Two hours fly by every single time I volunteer here at the pantry. It's amazing. The pantry is closing in two hours, so I will wait for my replacement volunteer to come before I leave.

"Hey Jenny, good to see you. You ready to take over for me?" I ask when I see Jenny walking towards me.

"Yep! How did everything go today?" Jenny asks me.

"Really good. I had no problems today, so that made for a great shift!" I say to her.

"Good work. Okay. See you next Friday!" Jenny tells me.

"Okay! See ya!" I grab my purse and jacket and say goodbye to Dennis and Kara.

I helped a lot of people today. But the one lady on my mind is Anna Maria. I mean, I've been crying like a baby and feeling sorry for myself over the past few months cause Jake is three hours away from me when people like Anna Maria, who just lost her husband, are in need of food. How selfish can I be? I mean, I've got what Zac calls "first-world problems," which are petty, childish problems. I mean yeah, they feel real to me, but today is the first day that reality has hit me, and I feel like a big, selfish baby!

I continue to mull over these thoughts in my mind as I drive home.

I need to talk with my mom about some of these thoughts I'm having when I get home—too many what-ifs and how-abouts with my dumb and selfish behavior while I was listening to Ana Maria's story. Mom will help me sort this stuff out.

I drive home in silence, which I'd like to point out isn't my normal behavior. Usually, I am rocking out anytime I drive. I mean like EVERY time. But today's experience has me feeling really off balance emotionally.

I'm still pondering things as I pull the car into the garage, get out, and walk into my beautiful, warm, and safe house through the garage entrance.

I look around to see who's home and, most of all, where my mom is right now, and see what she's doing. I hear voices coming from Mom and Kenneth's office. I softly knock on the door.

"Come in!" Mom's sweet voice calls out to me. I open the door and peek into the room. Mom and Kenneth are hard at work. *Dang it.*

"Hey Gracie Lou! What's up?" Mom asks me.

"Oh. Hey guys. I need to talk with you, Mom, when you're not busy," I say to both of them.

Kenneth answers me first. "We need about ten minutes, and then your mom is all yours!"

"Cool, k. I'll get some food and be back in ten." I close the door and retreat to the kitchen to get something to eat. It's as I enter my kitchen that I look at how big it is. How pretty it is. How much food do we have?

I feel sick to my stomach. I almost lose my appetite, but I'm actually too starved not to eat a little something. Dinner won't be for a few more hours, so I make a plate with cheese, crackers, and fruit and sit down at the table. I don't even scroll Insta while I eat. Nope. I just eat in silence.

How can I just be seeing all that I have right now? And why today? Why haven't I been seeing all of this before?

Ten minutes pass, and I clean up my snack plate and area and head to the office. I knock again.

"Come in Gracie!" Mom says to me. I open the door again and see that Kenneth is gone, and I walk towards my fave chair and plop down in it.

"Okay, gloomy Gus, what's up?" Mom asks me, looking at my sad face.

"Mom! Why haven't you busted me for being the most selfish human on earth?" I sigh.

"What in the world are you talking about, Gracie? You are NOT a selfish person. Where did you ever get that idea?"

"Today on my shift, the first client I helped was a sweet lady named Ana Maria- which for her privacy's sake, was a new client, and she told me that her husband died recently, and she's barely able to make it on her social security money per month, and she's got medical bills from her husband, so she came to get food! She was so sweet, and all I could think of was what my actual problem was— crying when Jake leaves, pouting when he's not around on his off weekend? Who am I thinking of? ME, only me." I actually started to cry at this point. The weight of all that I'm feeling is so heavy, like I'm carrying two large bags of sand on each shoulder. I can't help but cry. I feel so dumb and so selfish.

"Oh, honey, I'm sorry. How can I help you?" Mom asks.

"I feel so heavy. I feel like I can't walk because I feel so heavy. Does that even make sense?" I sniffle and wipe my cheeks.

"Absolutely makes sense, sweetie. I mean, you've always been a kind and compassionate person to your friends and family. And obviously, with your dad having passed away, you've experienced loss and sadness. But it seems like this experience today, and hopefully your experiences during your other shifts over the past few months, are teaching you that there is a great big world out there and that there are many real-life problems others have that you have never experienced and may never. I am surprised that Ana Maria shared as much with you as she did. She must have needed to talk with someone today, ya know?"

I don't answer immediately, but just nod my head. I'm thinking over what she's just shared with me.

"Okay, yeah, I am a nice person and I feel like I care about people, but I feel like my mind has just been selfishly full of ME thoughts, and that's all!"

"You are not selfish sweetie. You're just maturing and understanding life more at this time, which I feel is great. It's hard not to be self-absorbed at this age in your life. In fact, most of us are very selfish at some point in our young lives. I know I sure was! It's when you can start to see with different "eyes," so to speak, outside of yourself, that shines a light on the world around you and those living in it," Mom explains.

"Yeah, okay, I guess that makes good sense. I just feel like I've been knocked in the head with like a lot of clues, ya know?" I say.

"Actually, yes, I know just what you're saying. I had a similar experience when I was a few years older than you. Your dad and I were dating, and I worked as a writer for a small online news company. I was asked to cover a fire that had destroyed an entire apartment building due to faulty wiring, and well, I was devastated as I spoke with person after person and they shared with me their hard situation they were in now. Many were single moms. My heart broke. I wanted to help them all, but what could I do? I was just a 25-year-old. I could write about it."

She pauses then continues, "I asked my boss for permission to gather items for the tenants and got our little town to donate a lot of stuff. I felt so good having done just a little bit to help them. From that point on, your dad and I made sure we always gave money or items as much as we could afford to support various non-profits around us. Kenneth and I just started to talk about starting this up again."

I nod, fascinated.

"I don't know if you remember, but when you were younger, we would gather items, or I'd have you guys save some of your allowance. Then we'd take the donations or money to someone in need." Mom shares with me. "When your dad died, I couldn't think clearly for a long time, so that's why you might not remember us doing that. I was actually going to talk with everyone and see if anyone would join us in giving back to others this year, but I haven't had a chance as of yet. The whole movie deal got pushed back six months, which is just fine with me, but that gives me time now to talk with all of us."

"I totally remember that! Duh. Like, how did I forget that all? I know. Dad died. That's why. My heart was broken for a long time. All of our hearts were," I mutter softly.

"Exactly. But now your life has blossomed and bloomed, and you're in college and learning to draw and have sisters' night with Beth and have a terrific boyfriend. So, I feel you've finally healed enough to have space to open up your heart to others. I am so happy you chose to volunteer at the food pantry. Look at the experience you had today! It makes you see life differently. Doesn't mean you can't enjoy what you have, or have to sell off all you've got, just means you have room in your mind and heart to look outside of yourself and see who's around you," Mom says.

"Yeah, I guess you're right. Before Jake came into my life, and I guess even Brooke, I had zero to give because of my dad dying so suddenly. I didn't know if I could even feel happy again. Ugh. I almost hate thinking about that time, but it became a time to learn to be more compassionate and to understand loss and all that emotional stuff that comes with death, even if I didn't realize it. I've learned how to be unselfish with Jake in my life, I guess, too. And especially after the whole experience with Brooke last year, and how she was so freaking mean to me, and then her getting into that terrible accident and ending up in a coma, and then Brooke and I becoming friends after she apologized, I see that you're right. I see how I was able to forgive Brooke and care for her. I definitely showed compassion to her when I could have made a different choice, ya know?" I reply.

Mom beams. "Exactly. Today was another person for you to show compassion towards and to be aware of, as well as others you serve. I think, from this point on, you'll still miss Jake, but I can see that today was another experience that will change your heart and mind, so you'll be more focused on your volunteer shift and those you serve, hanging with Beth and us, and diving even deeper into your art. What do you think?"

"I think you're right, Mom. Thank you for taking the time to talk with me."

"Anytime, my dear Gracie Lou." Mom comes over to me from around her desk and embraces me. Oh, how I love my momma hugs. I nestle my face into her sweet-smelling hair and then pull back. We walk out together in silence. I feel so much better. Wow. My mom is just AMAZE. I don't know what I'd do without her. For real.

19

FEBRUARY

"Is this semester longer than the last one, or am I just making that up?" I ask Beth as I turn toward her. It's Tuesday: Sisters' Night.

"Oh, it's longer for sure. I swear, January was like three months rolled into one!" Beth laughs.

"Oh my gosh yes it was! Holy crud. Didn't think it would ever end!" I say, exasperated.

"Totally. But we made it to February, even though it's so freaking cold! February in Texas is so weird, right?" Beth observes.

"So weird. Our weather is so weird, in general, though. Sheesh. It can't make up its mind!" I laugh.

"For realz," Beth agrees. We are sitting in the dining room at the table making beaded wire decorations for Valentine's Day, which is next Tuesday.

I saw a tutorial last week on how to make them, and since the weather is so bad and we can't go to school tomorrow due to the ice freeze, we both decided that tonight's activity together would be to go all out and make decorations!

"Is Jake coming home this weekend or next?" Beth asks me while cutting out big pink hearts from construction paper.

"Next." I make a face.

"Sucks," Beth adds.

"Totally. But, hey, it's not the end of the world, just *almost* the end of the world," I snicker.

"Ha, yeah, I get it," Beth says.

"How's Ian? Did I already ask you if he's in any of your classes?" I inquire.

"It's cool, too much going on in our lives to remember everything going on with each other. But the answer is yes! Two classes. In fact, weather permitting, he'll come over Thursday night to study with me. He's so nice, Gracie. So cute, too, and smart," Beth cheerfully says.

"I'm sooooo glad for you. Sounds like Jake," I reply.

She grins. "Absolutely like Jake, and Alex is just as great. Meg is really digging him; in fact, they'll be joining us too on Thursday."

"I'm happy for you, girlies. I am so glad Jake and I were friends before dating and that we took it slowly, ya know? Man, I know of way too many girls who rush into a physical relationship, then the dude drops them like a hot potato," I say.

"Oh my gosh, me too! Forget that. My heart couldn't handle it. I like Ian. He's great, but we are definitely taking things slowly and getting to know one another and our families. And by families, I mean the siblings. What if I didn't like Sarah? Or Jake? That would so suck," Meg explains.

I totally agree with her. "Amen to all of that."

"I'm done with my bead decoration. What do you think?" Beth asks.

"Oh, it is really cute! We need to decide where we'd like to put our decorations now. Look! I'm almost done with mine." I hold it up for Beth to see.

"Oh yeah. Super cute," she tells me.

We have music playing as we work on our crafts. We are both happy to be out of school tomorrow, so we're relaxed and enjoying the pseudo fire, courtesy of our electric fireplace. It gives off real heat, so that's pretty cool. We decided earlier that we'd work on this stuff for about another hour, then watch a movie together. We're going to watch one of our faves: *Miss Congeniality* 'cause it's one of my family's favorite movies. We three kids grew up watching it because my dad loved this movie- that's why he named me Grace, after Sandra Bullock's character- Gracie Lou Freebush!

So funny! I plan to check in with Jake later on before bed. Oh, he did get accepted for the internship, and it's virtual, so that he can be here for the summer. I thought that was great. Notice how I'm not being all emotional? If he had to go somewhere, then that's what he'd do. And I could handle it without complaint.

Because every Friday, as I volunteer, I listen to so many sad and tragic stories about the experiences or struggles these people are facing or have faced. I am grateful that it has changed my heart. It's made me very thankful for my cushy life.

Okay, except for my dad passing, that was tragic, but I mean these days. If I have any problems, there are "First World Problems," as Jake calls them. And he's right. We don't have ANY real issues. More like inconveniences, is all.

Beth and I finished our movie around eleven pm. We laughed and laughed together! It was great. Mom and Kenneth are out of town this entire week, negotiating contracts, etc., and approving the actors and actresses for the movies based on books one through three.

It's so exciting! I'm ecstatic for my mom! She's been writing for years, so this is truly remarkable. She's worked on her book series for soooo long, too. Beth and I are holding down the house, with just the two of us.

I texted my mom earlier, telling her about the bad weather here in Texas. She said she'd seen it on the news (they're in New York) and asked if we were okay and if we had what we needed in case we were staying indoors for a few days. I told her we were fine.

Texas experiences unusual ice storms that typically occur in February. Beth and I head to bed, but first we open the under-the-sink doors and turn on a little drip from the kitchen faucet. We do the same in all three bathrooms. Pipes can freeze, so we're taking precautions. Having said our goodnights to each other, I jump on my bed and check my phone. No texts.

That's okay. I've been busy all day. I'll just check in with Jake and see how his day has been.

Gracie <hey, you what's up? Beth and I had the best night together. We made and put up so many Valentine decorations, and then we watched *Miss Congeniality*. It was great. Do you guys have ice like us?>

I see the bubble dots and know that Jake is responding.

Jake <hey beautiful girl, that sounds like a great night. Meg told me about the ice storm, yuck. We're good here, just cold>

Gracie <glad you don't have ice. We're off to school tomorrow, so Beth and I are having a *Twilight* movie marathon and making sugar cookies to decorate. Mom and Kenneth are in New York for the entire week. How have your classes been?>

Jake <oh yeah I remember you told me they had a week-long trip. Hope it goes well. Classes were good, hanging with the roomies tonight, and ordered in a Domino's college pizza deal while we study>

Gracie <so fun, good for you guys gotta get to bed, I'll check in tomorrow>

Jake <perf heart ya Gracie miss you>

Gracie <heart ya and '[

]miss you 2>

I begin my bedtime routine, and while I'm washing my face and brushing my teeth, I feel happiness within me for two reasons: one, Jake always makes me happy, and two, I didn't say anything about not being together for Valentine's Day, nor did I even feel weird emotions that Jake hadn't texted me first.

Yay for me! For once, I didn't let my emotions make up a story that wasn't true! I'm writing that in my journal for sure. It's a "Christmas miracle" that's for sure. I grab my journal, write a quick paragraph, then put it away and pick up my Kindle.

I'm loving my cozy mystery series I've been reading! They're so fun. I love to read before bed, and I love to have happy thoughts of Jake and my day while I drift off to sleep. Always a better way to end my day!

MARCH

"Um, excuse me? We're going where now, for Spring Break?" I say very loudly to my mom, who's literally standing right by me, haha. She's just told me some freaking awesome news.

"London!" My mom squeals with excitement.

"We wanted to surprise you girls for Spring Break this year," Kenneth says. He's always soft-spoken and kind. I just love that about him.

"Oh my gosh, I'm so excited I could cry! But, I won't, I'm so excited!" I say this twice 'cause I am so excited. Mom, Kenneth, Beth, and I are going to London for an entire week! I'm freaking out. That means next Monday!

"What made y'all think of doing this crazy surprise for us?" I ask them.

"Well, your mom has made some pretty great money since she and I signed all the documents and contracts for her movie deal, so we thought, why not?" Kenneth tells Beth and me.

"Holy! I'm sort of freaking out right now! I can't wait an entire week to go! LONDON!!!" Beth says giddily.

"Me too! I'm so excited. Wait. What should we pack for a trip to

London? I guess we will need to go shopping then to get travel clothes! Right mom? Darn, what a shame, Beth, am I right?" I tease.

"Absolutely. And you know I have to shop!!" Beth grins.

"Yes, girls. We've already figured this into the travel budget. Now, you know I've traveled a lot, as has Kenneth, so the best way to go is to have a mix-and-match wardrobe. Less is better. We bought you both international carry-on suitcases. Kenneth? Could you get those from my office, please, dear?" Mom says and turns to Kenneth.

"Of course. Hold on, girls." Kenneth smiles while walking to the office, and as he's rolling them out to us.

"Here you go! One silver. One black." Kenneth offers them to us.

"Silver, please," I say quickly.

"Black is good for me, then," Beth adds.

"They're so tiny! Sheesh," I comment, surprised.

"And therein lies the idea behind buying mix-and-match pants, sweaters, and shirts, and the 'less is better' concept. I say we grab a bite to eat here and get to the mall tonight. Let's see how we do in finding the right clothing items, and if we need to do more shopping, can we use sisters' night to finish?" Mom asks Beth and me.

"Uh, yes!" Beth and I say in unison.

"Okay, it's a plan. Girls, I also typed out some outfit ideas and pieces to buy." Mom hands us both a piece of paper.

We peruse it quickly.

"Not as bad as I was thinking it would be," Beth says.

"Agreed. Very doable. And we both have our Brooks and Hokas. So the shoes are already solved." I say agreeably.

"True. That helps a lot," Mom tells us. "Kenneth, are you up for whipping up some sandwiches right now? I'd like to take the girls to our room and show them a couple of items they can buy when we go out shopping."

"Of course, sweetie. Give me fifteen minutes, ladies, and the meal will be ready!" Kenneth tells us as we walk to the kitchen.

"Thanks, Kenneth!" both Beth and I chime in at the same time. Again!

We follow Mom into their room. She has some outfit ideas laid out on her bed. We all three take time to look at the items and chat about the clothes, and then discuss which stores will work best. Athleta. ALO and Under Armor to start with. And def Uniqlo.

Kenneth calls to us and we leave their bedroom, chatting all the way to the kitchen. He has made us all sandwiches, chips, and grapes with water or milk to drink. Delish. We scarf everything down, clean up, and head to the garage. We need to get in since we both still have school all week.

THE SHOPPING SPREE ACTUALLY WAS A HUGE SUCCESS. AND WE GOT ALL we needed, and we will use our existing items of clothing from our wardrobes. Beth and I opened our suitcases and put them on the floor of our bedroom, then started packing.

I got a few colorful scarves to wear around my neck if the weather is cool at all. Apparently, that's a way to add color to a neutral traveling wardrobe. Works for me! I bought a simple pack of silver hoops to wear each day. And plan to wear my hair in braids or up on a ponytail. Beth's hair is a little shorter, so she'll stick to headbands and two buns or half up, half down. We see both so giddy we can't hardly settle down. I've been itching to text Jake more info now that we went shopping.

He was so happy about our upcoming trip. He'll come home and spend time with his family, and then he and Meg will fly out to see their mom in California. I hope that goes well.

Gracie < hey you just got back from the mall, and Beth and I found all the things that we needed for London. To say that we are excited is an understatement. I've never been out of the country, and I've always wanted to go to London>

Jake < that's great, Gracie. I'm glad you guys were able to do that, especially since you have only a few days before you leave. Meg and I will fly out next Thursday night.

We're going to spend Friday and Saturday with my mom and return before you come home, and then I'll leave for school again on

Sunday. I'm glad you're going to be back Saturday night so that we can hang out Sunday together before I leave>

Gracie < me too. I hope your trip goes well. I hope you both have a good visit with your mom>

Jake < ngl, I'm a little nervous, but worst case, Meg and I can book a trip home earlier if things aren't going well, but I am thinking positively and my mom genuinely sounds excited to have us both come and stay, so that's good>

Gracie < oh, good, that makes me feel better. I was wondering what her reaction was when you asked if you guys could fly out to visit her in California>

Jake < yeah, like I said, I didn't know if she would be cool with it, I mean, we've kept up texting and sometimes we'll talk on the phone same with Meg but a little hesitant because you know her little heart has been broken by her mom leaving obviously, but she does Face-Time and they text and mom and continues to go to therapy just helping her work through everything and also will help her before we see our mom>

Gracie <oh good I'm so glad Beth gives me info here and there about Meg, but I appreciate you giving me updates on her and how she's doing. I've got therapy on Friday and then we fly out on Saturday>

Jake < speaking of therapy, you know how I said I felt OK and didn't need it? Well, I actually think I may need to talk to someone, so I found that they have counselors on campus here, so I'm gonna start going to see this guy named Dr. Hank when I come home from California>

Gracie < what? Oh, I'm so glad, Jake. I mean, I know you're tough, you're strong. You have a clear mind and understand how things work, but I'm with you. When emotions and hard situations get too big, I have to see a therapist so I can figure out how to deal with them. Deal with it all.>

Jake < yeah, that's where I'm at. Had a good talk with Robert the other day, and he suggested that I go talk to someone. He said it's OK to be tough and cool and all that stuff, but it's not OK to suffer, so I agreed with them, and just cause I'm a dude doesn't mean I can't go to therapy.>

Gracie < Ha, you're correct, and I'm super proud of you for identifying this—seriously! OK, I'd better get ready for bed! Have a great sleep, and I'll text you tomorrow. *Heart* ya>

Jake <sleep well *heart* ya back>

In case you haven't noticed, Jake and I have been putting "*heart* ya" at the end of our texts for the last few months. Very cool! And so cute!! Right? It makes my heart flutter like butterfly wings! I love it. K, really, I'm getting ready for bed! A few more days, then London! Oh yeahhhhhhhhh!!!

I forgo the journal and the Kindle, and opt for my AirPods and put on my beach waves list so I can just go to sleep quickly!

Dear Journal,

LONDON was incredible! We hit every historical landmark: the Tower of London, Buckingham Palace, the London Eye, and Big Ben. Then we went to Westminster Abbey, Tower Bridge, and St. Paul's Cathedral. It was incredible! Like, I can't even with how amazing it was! We walked and walked and ate and ate. We took trains, and we saw every touristy spot possible. It was incredible! We bought a few souvenirs, too, but there wasn't a lot of room, so we were careful about what we purchased.

The wardrobe was perfection. Beth and I were warm on cold days and cool on warmer days. We're already planning another trip next spring!

Jake and Meg: their trip was okay, but super hard. I got a phone call from Jake letting me know their mom is very mentally unwell, but apparently, she's going to see a psych to see if she needs to take some meds, and then she says she'll be starting some talk therapy. Jake was pretty upset- which I don't blame him. Mental illness is no joke, and boy how it affects the person mentally ill AND their family members!

It's like I've figured out since being in therapy for a long while: everyone needs to go to talk therapy! For realz. They did stay the entire time, but it was rough a few times. Meg was upset a few times, but Jake told me he helped her work through her frustration, which was a good thing.

I am exhausted! Jake and Meg, Beth, Mom, Kenneth, and I had a fabulous Sunday funday! We played so many games of UNO- it was very thera-

peutic for ALL of us. And we laughed and ate rice krispie treats and pizza! Sighhhh, and as I am writing this, my heart is sad because my Jake just left! Ugh. Plus, I need to get some sleep before classes start tomorrow. Oh! I took a small sketchbook with me and drew a lot. It was really great! I'll bring it to class on Tuesday and show it to Ms. Valeria.

I also added back in Spanish as a course. Working at the food pantry is showing me I need to know Spanish wayyyy better, so I'm going to go year-round to become proficient. I'm actually pretty excited. Just the other day, five of my ten clients spoke Spanish! Holy! I need to get on it!

Adios! Gotta get some sleep!

XOXOXOXOXO

21

APRIL

Mom < on Easter Sunday, I'd like to have Jake and his family join us. Zac and Sarah will be in town, too. Could you ask Jake if that works for them? We still have two weeks before Easter Sunday, but you know, I want to be ready, and Kenneth needs to know how many mouths to feed lol>

Gracie <for sure! I'm on my way home from art class! Are you at the house? If so, see you in ten minutes!>

Mom <yep! I'm here>

Gracie <k>

While I am driving home, my thoughts suddenly dart to the end-of-the-month art show!

I am really getting nervous! Which of my projects should I even put in the show?

I am stressed big time. We've done so many projects since last semester, too, and over the past two months, we've been exploring colors and paint, and I have come to love both gouache and acrylics. Painting is soooooo wonderful! I thought I loved drawing!

Well, now that we've added painting to our projects, it has been literally AMAZING! Ms. Valeria has a specific order that you need to follow to complete projects: sketch/draw in pencil, outline in Sharpie, and add paint.

Also, I've discovered these things called acrylic paint markers, and they're incredibly fun to use. One of our classmates showed us all, and Ms. Valeria was like ummm, everyone needs to get a set! So, "thanks, Amazon," I ordered mine today! When they come, I'll be sure to show my family, because they're sooo much fun to use.

Need to go and visit with my mom! Have some tea to share with her.

I walk down the stairs and immediately start to call her name.

"Mom? Where are you?" I figure mom is probs in her office, but I like to call her name anyway!

"Here Gracie! Office," she calls out to me.

"Hey there! I mentioned my end-of-the-month art show, didn't I? We're to pick five pieces to put on exhibit. Needless to say, I'm officially freaked out!" I say as I go to sit down.

"Oh yes, yes, I do remember that. Okay, so did you ask Ms. Valeria for some help in choosing which ones to show?" Mom asks.

"I mean, not outright. I guess I can do that on Thursday. We've got three weeks to show time, and we've got five more classes to go before the show. I'll look tonight after work. Oh, I asked Jake about Easter Sunday and he gave me a resounding yes, haha, and asked if his dad could bring a lady friend named Christy, too?" I wonder how Mom will react to that revelation.

"Of course. Hmmmm. Who's this Christy person?" Mom makes her 'tell me more' face.

I just laugh. "All Jake said was they knew each other in college, and she's recently divorced, like him. Crazy how that stuff works in life, isn't it?"

"For sure. Well, the answer again is, of course, and we look forward to meeting her," Mom says.

"She's got a daughter who's the same age and grade as Meg and Beth. How cool is that? I hope she's nice, though," I reply.

Mom nods. "Okay, that is cool, and I agree. That sweet family needs NICE."

"K, cool, and thanks for having everyone over!" I glance at my watch. "Time for me to get ready for work! Bye, I'll be home after 6:00 pm."

"Bye, sweetie. See you for dinner." I wave goodbye to Mom as I leave her office, walk down the hall, and go up the stairs.

Later tonight, Beth and I will be making nameplate cards for Easter and a few decorations. We've really enjoyed our "crafty nights" together.

We will have a large group for Easter (Jake, Meg, Samuel, Christy, her daughter, Zac, Sarah, Mom, Kenneth, Beth, and me—12 people), which is the way we like it! I had mentioned to Beth that we could go to the craft store and see if they have any cute nameplate holders.

So, when I'm done with my shift tonight, I'll drive home and pick her up, and then we can cruise around the store to find some items for our Easter Sunday dinner fiesta!

Speaking of my shift, I ended up talking with Dennis and Kara at the food pantry at the end of my shift, and it seems they'll need to hire a full-time employee for the summer. They asked me to consider applying. I was really surprised and flattered.

I have just been working extra hard at my volunteering shifts, not realizing that I was catching the interest of both Dennis and Kara. I am glad they spoke with me today because

I've been really thinking hard about how much I love volunteering at the Food Pantry, and now this potential job could be a stepping stone to what I've been thinking about over the past few months.

I researched the Public Health degree, and I believe it will be a good fit for me to pursue as my Bachelor's degree, allowing me to focus on Health and Nutrition for communities after I obtain my associate's degree.

Blast! I forgot to talk with Mom about a potential new job opportunity. I'll talk to her later on this week about it.

"Oooo, Beth, look at these? Those are super cute, right?" I'm pointing to these tiny bunnies in a basket with a slot to hold nameplates.

"Oh yeah, those are adorbs. Let's get those." Beth hands me one at a time until we've got twelve.

"Maybe, let's get two more just in case one breaks?" Beth suggests.

"Oh, yeah, great idea. Okay, I see some cute placemats, as well as some napkins to match. Ooooo, let's get some napkin rings. Oh, these are sooo cute!" I am literally walking down the aisles, pulling things out, and flinging them into our grocery cart. I look at Beth to see her give me such a big, dramatic eye roll.

"Hey! This dinner is a big deal. New lady for Mr. Hansen? Possible new stepsister for Jake and Meg? Big stuff, Beth. Big stuff." I laugh, but I'm totally serious. Beth is a good sport and goes along with me as we continue down aisle after aisle.

"Um, Gracie Lou, thinking we've got all we need, yeah?" she asks with a pleading tone.

"Yes! Thanks for going along with me, little sis. Okay, let's check out and get home so we can get on making the nameplates." I tell her as I wheel the cart, and we get into a line. "I forgot to tell you, I grabbed some nice cardstock paper we can cut apart to make the nameplates. Does that work for you?"

"Oh yeah, good idea. And I got some nice black markers for us, too." Beth says.

"Good idea! Thanks." I pay for our items, and Beth and I grab our bags and head for the exit. It's only 7:30 pm, so we've got enough time to start and still get to bed on time.

One thing I do before sisters' night is complete all my homework on Mondays. Beth gets her stuff done after school while I'm at work.

We load up the Lexus and get in the car. While I buckle my seatbelt, Beth queues up our playlist. We rock out all the way home, talking together. I sure love this sister of mine. She's become very special to me—more than she used to be.

It's nice to be closer nowadays. I'm super happy about this extra benefit of attending our local community college. I pull the car into the garage, and we grab our purchases, eager to show Mom and Kenneth before Beth and I get to work on our craftivity. We get a lot of oh's and ah's from them, making both Beth and me happy with our choices.

We get to work and end up making the nameplates until about

9:30 pm-ish, because we've added a lot of flourishing to each one. We decided that one more Tuesday will get everything done, so that's our plan for next Tuesday's sisters' night.

Easter Sunday is at the end of next week, so we have plenty of time. Jake will be home, and we get to meet Christy and her daughter. Oh, what the heck is her name? I've got to remember to ask Jake when I text him before bed tonight. We need her name for the nameplate!

"C A L L I E, Callie," I tell Beth. She's got amazingly straight and beautiful writing, so she started the nameplates and is finishing them tonight now that we know the daughter's name is Callie.

I painted little flowers on the nameplates first so that Beth could write them out when they dried. I must admit, they're incredibly adorable. Beth and I make a stellar team, if I do say so myself!

Mom bought a new, larger tablecloth for the dining room table so that we can extend it on Sunday. We still need to add a few more items to the menu: ham, twice-baked potato casserole with bacon pieces, a green salad, and a fruit salad. Kenneth is also making teeny carrot cakes for dessert. It all sounds so freaking delicious! I can't wait!

Meanwhile, I did end up talking to Ms. Valeria last week. I waited for her after class, and thankfully, she had a good hour before her next class to help me.

"Hey, Ms. Valeria, can I ask you for some help with deciding which art pieces I should choose for the art show? I'm pretty nervous to show everyone my projects." I say to her, lowering my eyes.

"But Gracie, you're so good at art! So very good." I raise my eyes in total shock and surprise!

"You really think so?"

"Absolutely! I see how you've improved from the start to now! I see how you can follow pictures and can recreate them so well, and your color choices are beautiful! Let me see your portfolio, and I can help you choose." I smile, feeling a wave of relief wash over me. I pull my portfolio out and spread my projects out. She helps me decide on a few art projects I've already completed, and then we discuss how I can add two more from our upcoming projects.

I come away feeling less nervous and proud of myself: from stick figures to actual art! Cool. Very cool.

I know I've been talking about Easter coming, and that's because we are meeting CALLIE for the first time!! So when it is finally Easter Sunday, I am happy and looking forward to later on today!

My family and I attend church from 10:30 am to 12:30 pm, and then rush home to prepare all the food and decorations and get everything ready. Festivities start around 4:00 pm. We plan to have some appetizers, visit, and then eat.

"Hey girls! I need you!" Mom calls Beth and me from downstairs. Beth and I first ran upstairs to quickly change out of our church clothes into more casual clothing, but still looked nice for the day.

"Coming!" Beth responds.

"Me too!" I chime in.

My mind has been on this girl, Callie. What is she going to be like? Will she mesh with Jake and Meg? Visions of the very typical Cinderella story I've ever read or watched in a movie from the past fly through my mind: stepsisters usually suck, and stepmoms, too!

Crap. I hope she proves me wrong today! I hope Christy is nice, too! Ugh. Jake hadn't met either one of them until last night. He came in later Saturday night this weekend because he had a class project he needed to finish and turn in.

I haven't heard from him today, so I have zero info about either one. I'm sort of freaking out FOR them!

"Mom? What do you want Beth and me to do?" I ask her as soon as I enter the dining room.

"Oh, hey, thanks for coming down so quickly. Will you and Beth handle the table setup since you two did such a wonderful job and made adorable decorations and the nameplates?" Mom replies.

"Of course! We wanted to do that anyway." I say. "Beth? Let's go!"

"I'm on it! Chill!" Beth grumps.

"Okay, okay! Sheesh!" I respond.

I think she's stressed about Callie too, cause Beth is never rude! Like never! I'll talk with her while we set everything up. I mean, Meg is her best friend, and I know Beth doesn't want any more heartache for her.

Kenneth and I put in the table leaves. Then he scurries back to the kitchen like a busy little chipmunk gathering its nuts. I then get the new, pale yellow tablecloth and spread it out over the entire, very large table.

We can fit fourteen people when we add in both leaves; it's such a great table! I drag a few other chairs into the dining room to add to the existing chairs already around the table. Then I roll every napkin and put each one into a bunny napkin holder.

"These are soooo cute!" I say aloud to myself. I hear Beth coming down the stairs. Rapidly.

She looks flustered when she comes into the dining room area.

"Hey Beth, what's up? You seemed a little bugged when I called up to you!" I say as she walks in.

"I'm so sorry, Gracie! I was texting back and forth with Meg. Callie and her mom are due to arrive in just a few minutes, and Meg is freaking out and for real, freaking out. I tried to reassure her. I don't think I did that one bit. Fingers crossed their initial meeting goes okay!" Beth explains to me.

"I knew it! Crap. Sorry, Beth. Let's hope it goes well. So stressful. Seriously. Hate this for them, but maybe we will be pleasantly surprised?" I try to reassure Beth.

"Yeah, maybe, anyway, what can we do about it other than wait and see them in an hour!" Beth says.

"Yeah, totes. K, subject change: nameplates, and then let's sprinkle the Easter confetti down the middle, how about? Mom has a few small vases of flowers, and we can also put them down the middle," I suggest.

"Yeah, all sounds good," she responds.

We work steadily for about 30 minutes and have the table looking amazing. Place settings, glasses, we even have those charger plates (didn't know we owned those or what they were used for until today -

you put them under the actual plate to make it all look more fancy, haha), and all the silverware.

Kenneth and Mom plan to set all the food in the kitchen so everyone can grab their plate and then go into the kitchen and go down the line and get what they'd like to eat. Easier than dishing everyone up.

Beth and I head towards the kitchen after a last look at our table setup.

"Hello! We're done. What about you guys?" I ask Mom and Kenneth.

"Yep! Just timing a few more things so we can eat by 5:00 pm. Zac just texted me and said he and Sarah will be here closer to 5:00 pm. Beth, could you please grab the hors d'oeuvres from the outside fridge? Gracie, will you help me make this drink? The ingredients and recipe are over on the kitchen table," Mom asks us both.

"Yep!" Beth says.

"On it," I add.

Before we know it, the doorbell is ringing. Beth and I look at each other. Our eyes say what our mouths don't: ready or not, here we go! We paste on our best smiles, link arms, and head to the front door.

Greetings are exchanged, so Beth leads everyone into the family room. I find Jake in the group to see what his face looks like.

He's definitely smiling. That's a good sign.

I then look for Beth and Meg, and I see a girl who must be Callie standing by a pretty, dark-haired lady whom I assume is Christy, because Mr. Hansen is standing next to her and they're holding hands.

She's pretty and how sweet! They're holding hands.

Jake walks over to me and gives me a big hug and a kiss on my cheek.

"Well, hello, beautiful girl!" he says.

I instantly blush. "Hi! Good to see you!"

"Let me introduce you to Callie and Christy." Jake takes my hand and leads me over to his dad and Christy.

"Grace, this is Christy Black. Christy, this is my girlfriend, Grace." Jake introduces us, and Christy stands up.

"Oh, I am so glad to meet you! I've never heard a boy talk about a girl as much as Jake talks about you!" she says and pulls me into a hug.

"Oh, ha, he's too kind to me! It's so nice to meet you, Christy," I reply, smiling. Jake continues to lead me, and this time we head to the other couch where Beth, Meg, and Callie are all chatting together like little squirrels in a park. They're all smiling, so I'm taking that as another good sign.

"Callie, this is my girlfriend, Gracie. Beth is her little sister," Jake says to Callie. Callie also stands up to meet me. *They're both polite. I like it.*

"Hey, Grace, it's nice to meet you! I'm Callie, but I, uh, I guess you already knew that, duh, sorry. I'm a little nervous. So many new things are happening this weekend, ya know?" She gives us a shy smile.

"It's all good. I'm glad to meet you, Callie. How old are you and what year in school?" I ask.

"I'm a sophomore and I'll be 16 in August," Callie answers.

"Oh, sweet, so exactly like Beth and Meg. Cool," I tell her.

"I know! Right? I was like Wow, that's a cool coincidence," Callie says.

"And y'all are in Washington?" I ask Callie.

"Uh, yeah, the Tacoma area. I guess my mom and Meg's dad knew each other in college a long time ago. I don't even know how they reconnected, but I'm cool with it. Samuel is so kind!" Callie gushes.

"Yeah, Jake was telling me that the other day. Well, welcome!" I say to her and smile as Jake and I walk away to find a place to sit. But the doorbell rings, and then the door opens, and in walk Zac and Sarah!

"My long-lost brother!" I run to him and give him a huge hug. And Sarah, too. "I've missed you both so much!"

"Us too! I'm so glad we can be here with everyone today! Hey Jake!" Zac calls.

"Zac! What's up, dude? So glad you guys are here!" Jake says enthusiastically.

Eventually, everyone finds a place to sit. The hors d'oeuvres are set out on the large coffee table. There's a comforting buzz of conversation I hear as we all start to visit and eat. Before long, Kenneth calls us all together, and we say a group prayer. He then blesses the food and welcomes Christy and Callie. Then we began the Easterpalooza eat-a-thon. The rest of the evening is filled with food, fun, conversation, and laughter.

I'm so excited that Jake has Monday off, so we plan to spend part of the day together. Sadly, Christy and Callie will be flying home to Washington tomorrow, so that Mr. Hansen will take them later on to the airport.

I really liked them both so much. They fit right in with all of us! Callie was kind and sweet. Beth was nervous for Meg, cause it's not easy welcoming new potential family members.

I'll be sure to tell Jake how much I liked both Callie and Christy when I text him in a bit. It seemed like both Jake and Meg were cool with Callie and Christy, too, because we all played games together, and there didn't seem to be any tension between Callie, Jake, and Meg. I'll check in with him on how he's feeling about all of this with his dad and Christy. This is a big change. As they continue dating, there could be some more permanent changes for Jake and his family.

I'm pondering this all as I finish writing in my journal. Then I pick up my phone to text Jake.

Jake <good night, right?>

Gracie <the best. I can't believe how much I like Christy and Callie. I was nervous. ngl>

Jake <Meg and I were so nervous. My dad seems genuinely happy. Who knows what will happen, but it's nice to know that Christy is nice and likes my dad, ya know?>

Gracie <absolutely! Phew. That's really all I can say. I'm glad today was good>

Jake <oh forgot to ask when our art show is?>

Gracie <next Thursday night>

Jake <dang, I was hoping it was on the weekend. I would have come>

Gracie <and I appreciate that really, but no worries. I'll have Kenneth make a video, how about? He's really good at that type of stuff>

Jake <that would be so good, thanks, I'm so tired, heading to bed. Oh, when are you done with your classes tomorrow again?>

Gracie <I'll be home by 1:00 pm>

Jake <okay, cool, let's have lunch, then I'll pack up and head out>

Gracie <sound perfect *heart* ya sleep well!>

Monday passed too quickly. Jake and I went to the movies early in the day and then went for an early lunch so we could say goodbye to Christy and Callie before they flew out.

AND BEFORE I KNEW IT, JAKE WAS ON HIS WAY BACK TO AUSTIN LATER that evening.

Sigh. Love that boy and love to have him around. Yeah, I've done way better at being less emotional, but saying goodbye will never be easy for me. But it's okay, because I need to get ready for Thursday night.

"GRACIE! YOU'RE A REALLY GREAT ARTIST. I'M SUPER IMPRESSED. Especially from your stick figure days!" Mom laughs. She has such an adoring look on her face.

I feel proud of myself. "I know, Mom, I mean, when I say there was a locked part of me, I just let loose, I am not kidding! Oh! Guys, come and meet Ms. Valeria!" I motion to Beth, Meg, Kenneth, and Mom to follow me. "Ms. Valeria, this is my family. My stepdad, Kenneth, my mom, my sister Beth, and her bestie Meg. Guys, this is Ms. Valeria!"

"Z pleasure iz all mine-uh," Ms. Valeria says. "Grace is a terrific artist."

I blush when she says this.

"I am very impressed with all you've taught her and how good Grace is as an artist!" Mom says proudly.

"She is a natural! I am very proud of her progress this year," Ms. Valeria replies as she gestures for us to walk around and see the other students' projects. I introduced everyone to a few of my classmates.

Kenneth takes a video of the evening, following me around and making me laugh—he's so great—and I will send it to Jake when I get home.

Driving home together, I fall into a really happy state. I am quiet. I am tired, but in a good way. I really stressed about this and am glad it's over, but I feel great about my efforts and all that I've learned.

I want to keep going with art classes. I know I've said this before, but who knew that art could help me as much as it has in regulating my emotions? I am utterly amazed at how it has changed my very soul.

IT'S LATE, SO I AM HURRYING THROUGH MY NIGHTLY ROUTINE, AND AS I crawl into my bed feeling a happy exhaustion, I send the video to Jake.

Gracie <great night, here's the video Kenneth made >

I figured Jake might not be able to respond as it was pretty late, but I sent the video anyway. As I just about to lay my head down and drift off to sleep, with the potential of having really sweet dreams, I hear my phone buzz.

Jake <GRACIE I am sooooo impressed with your art! WOW. You've only shown me a few of your drawings so it was AWESOME to see all of your work!! Great job. For real. Super proud of you>

Gracie <oh thanks so much! I hope I didn't interrupt you, I know it's kinda late. Appreciate your kind words>

Jake <heart ya>

Gracie <heart ya back>

22

MAY

"ALMOST DONE, Beth! We're almost freaking DONE!" I practically shout at her when I see her. It's our last sisters' night of the semester, and we decided we needed to get out of the house and get ice cream. We've got this delicious new ice cream place called Handel's that just came to our little city. It's really good. The weather is warming up every day. Not summer hot, but it's pleasant. We Texans pray for rain in the spring to bring us less heat in the summer. Yeah, it's a Texas thing.

We are all at the end of May, finishing up our finals. Jake will be home next week. Beth, Meg, Ian, and Alex have been studying for two weeks; I've been studying so much, too, as has Jake.

Jake didn't come home last weekend. Instead, he's just pushing through and will be home all summer next week. YAY!!!!! I can't wait. I accepted the position at the Food Pantry. I will start the second week of June, giving me an ENTIRE free week all to myself to hang with Jake before he starts his job. I'm super glad we can have a week off before we jump into summer jobs!

My art class finished last week (giving me sufficient time to study for finals). Mom and Kenneth are planning to be gone for the entire month of June. Beth and Meg got hired at Sicily's Pizza and will work there all summer.

Zac and Sarah are staying full-time at college because they're getting jobs and just living their lives in the Dallas area now. So much change! I can't even believe how much things have changed!

I'm glad I'm working on this now, though. My therapist has given me monthly homework: whenever I encounter any stressors or big emotions about something, I write them down on little pieces of paper and stuff them into a jar I found in the kitchen cupboard.

The action of writing it out and putting it physically into a jar helps me to take that stress away or that emotion away from me, and then I try not to let it creep up into my mind again—yeah, I know, it still happens, but it's been a good practice. Also, doing art every day is something I have been drawn to.

It's been pretty cool. This is also how I plan to keep up with my art this summer. I can't take a class because I will be working full-time, so I decided to do art every day instead. It's another thing that has helped me channel any extra energy or feelings I have.

I reach the swing set. I sit down and start to see. The weather is coolish with a light breeze, one of my fave types of Texas weather. I close my eyes while I swing and let myself drift back to when it all began three years ago with Jake. I remember it as if it were just yesterday…

"So are you up for ice cream and a walk in a park?"

"Oh, Jake, you don't have to buy me anything else, really. Dinner, a book, and now ice cream? Seriously, Jake, I'm good, you are spending too much money on me, or us, and I don't want to seem ungrateful, cause I really do appreciate it."

"Relax, Gracie, I wouldn't spend my money if I didn't want to. Promise. I have a lot of savings right now, so no worries, okay?"

"Okay, sure, I guess if you say so."

"Where to?"

"Have you tried Braum's yet?"

"Nope, but I'm game, so let's go! I trust your opinion completely."

He gives me a melt-in-my-mouth smile, and we are off.

We travel in silence for a while, listening to Metric, one of my favorite groups.

"I love Metric," I say with my eyes closed. I sing along softly.

"You know this?"

"Well, yeah, my brother Zac and I share a lot of tunes, and we all like music in my family."

"That's great." A fabulous smile flashes my way. Be still, my heart!

"You have a nice voice, Gracie."

"Thanks," I say shyly and turn my face towards the window. We decide to go through the drive-through so we can walk and eat in the park.

Ice cream purchased: Rocky Road for Jake and Peppermint for myself. We head towards a park close to my neighborhood to finish eating.

"Great ice cream, I mean seriously!"

"Right??" I beam. Peppermint ice cream and Jake Hotty? Life doesn't get better than this.

We both laugh as Jake pulls into an empty spot, then runs to my side to let me out. Once again, chivalry is not dead with Jake around.

I breathe in the pleasant smells as we walk towards the swings. It's slightly cooler than earlier in the day, refreshing, not frigid.

We both grab a swing and start to pump as we finish eating our ice cream. As we sail back and forth, I look over at Jake when I think he's not looking. This boy is beautiful, kind, and a lot of fun. Pinch me 'cause I'm dreaming the best darn dream ever!

"Um, Jake? Can I tell you something?" I slow my swing so I can look right at Jake.

"Sure." He follows my lead and slows down as well. We both stop. I look over at him.

"I can honestly say, this has been the most relaxing time I've had, well, since my dad died. I've been working, studying, and working even more, while also taking care of things around the house and taking care of Beth, Zac, and me for a long, long time. I never go out, actually, never." I breathe a sigh of relief and fall silent.

I peek at him again to see what his facial expression could be after my rando confession. I don't usually act like this, but this guy makes me feel relaxed, free, and allows me to be myself. I love feeling this way.

"I'm glad, Gracie." He winks at me. And that's that. He starts to pump again. I follow his lead now. He starts to ask me questions.

"How's it been since you lost your dad?"

"So hard at first. Really hard. Then, as the days became weeks and the weeks became months, things slowly became less hard. Less heart-wrenching. We fell into daily routines, subconsciously split up dad's jobs, and continued to move forward."

"That's good to hear, and I'm really glad to hear that it has gotten easier and better. I'm sorry it was so hard for you all, though."

"We have a wall in our dining room dedicated to Dad. Childhood pictures, awkward middle school years, and high school photos. Mom and Dad when they were dating, and their wedding. We were all babies with dad and mom, and then their last anniversary photo, before he died."

"I would love to see your Dad-wall sometime."

"I would love to show you. I, um, I don't ever talk about this with anyone. Not even my BFF Clara. So thank you for listening."

Speaking of Jake, my phone pings, and guess who? My cute boy.

Jake < Hey, you, what's up? Missing you, so I wanted to text>

Gracie <you'll never guess where I am right now or what I'm thinking of??>

Jake <where?>

Gracie <the park is by my house. I was thinking of our first date and what a nervous wreck I was, and how you still pushed forward and didn't give up on this girl who'd never been out with a boy before!>

Jake <and how glad I am that I didn't give up on you>

Gracie < I was thinking how I couldn't believe you liked books, and that you let me talk about my dad, and that I told you I write poetry okay, well maybe not poetry but free verse thoughts- which I share with no one but my journal ha ha!>

Jake <it was such a good night. I knew I'd made the right choice to get to know you better. Look at us now? Three years later, and you and I are about to finish our first year of college!>

Gracie <literally what I was just thinking about! The changes in our lives. Some good. Some hard and not-so-good>

Jake < Yeah, true. But mostly good, and look at you! An artist, smashing your grades, and I love that you and Beth have done sisters' night all year. I'm going to do that with Meg this summer. She's missed me and I've missed her—a lot>

Gracie <it was such a good idea for us to do this, and even though I hate to admit this openly, I don't regret staying home. I don't regret building a better rapport with Beth, my mom, and Kenneth. I don't regret going to community college. Nor do I regret taking my art classes.

I don't regret volunteering each week; in fact, it's been the BEST. Now I'm going to work there, and I know what I want to study for my bachelor's degree. I feel as if, well, I don't know how to say this, I feel like it was meant to be for me not to get into UT Austin. Does that sound weird?>

Jake <not one bit and I hate to admit it too, cause I seriously missed you every dang day, but I've seen you grow. I've seen you chill out emotionally (don't get mad, ha ha), I've seen you learn new things and push yourself to do art and volunteering all on your own, and I've seen you become such a better Gracie, and even though we have another dumb year of this, I look forward to seeing and hearing about the new experiences you'll be involved in>

I drink in his words like drinking a full glass of cold, chocolate milk that makes my stomach happy. This boy is something else. This boy of mine is I don't even have the words for him - he gets me, he believes in me, he encourages me, I mean, what more could a girl ask for?

Gracie < you're too sweet to me, really, thank you, and I'm not mad, you're right, I have chilled out, and I'm working on that more and more. Therapy has helped me so, so much. And volunteering has seriously changed me. I have listened to story after story of people's lives that are wrecked; they're sad; they're hungry, and I realized in January that I needed to get a grip and think of other people STAT>

Jake < Well, I've seen that change in you. Not like you weren't already kind or thoughtful, cause you were and are, but I see how this has helped you to think of others more, ya know? >

Gracie <yep, totally. Thanks again for your kind words, really. You're always so good to me>

Jake <You're easy to be kind to, Gracie Lou>

Gracie <before I forget to ask you, how is your studying going? I know you've got a lot of finals this week>

Jake <good actually and thankfully. Robert and I have been in the library for nearly two weeks. Tomorrow through Saturday, we have our finals, then plan on racing home to see you Saturday night!>

Gracie < I can't hardly wait! Finally! *Heart*>

Jake <goodnight, beautiful girl, and good luck on your finals, too! (are you home yet?)>

Gracie <yeah, I started walking back while we were texting- I'm in my bed, texting my favorite person! Goodnight!>

Jake < *Heart* >

EPILOGUE

I SPENT another year at the local community college, making a total of two years to earn my associate's degree. Staying around for another year enabled Beth and me to continue our sisters' nights every Tuesday. I signed up for another year of art classes with Ms. Valeria. Amazing classes! I am becoming a better artist, so that rocks.

Since Beth could take college classes from the community college, as a junior in High School, Beth can now earn extra credit for college. We end up taking a few classes together on Mondays and Wednesdays.

Oh! Exciting news! Ian and Beth are officially dating. Ian is at the house a lot, and Meg is dating his best friend, Alex. So they're also at the house a lot, too! I reapplied to UT Austin after discovering that it has a great Public Health program. I was accepted for my Bachelor's degree, which means... Jake and I can FINALLY go to college together!

I end up surprising both my family and Jake with the news that I have been accepted for my Associate's degree after graduation. Jake was BEYOND excited! He confessed to me that two more years without me on the same college campus was NOT his idea of FUN!

I continue to work at the food pantry. I became a full-time

employee the first summer after my freshman year in college, then continued to work part-time throughout my second year of college. Then I resumed full-time work again before Jake and I head off to UT Austin—together this fall. Oh, how I love the sound of those words: TOGETHER!!!!

Zac and Sarah got married in early August, a few weeks before Jake and I leave for our junior years in college.

Brooke and Justin ended up breaking up after their sophomore year, but Brooke met this great guy named James, who happens to know Jake's other roommates. So there's a connection. Justin moved on, too, and met a lovely girl named Marlow. Both Brooke and Justin continue to date their new significant others and are aiming to get married after everyone graduates from college. Luckily, Justin and Brooke stay friends, as do we all.

Mom and Kenneth are working on a deal to have all of her books made into movies. Kenneth is very busy keeping everyone fed when they are all home for visits and supporting Mom with her movie deals. Mom has finally finished book ten of her series, and then she decided to step away and take a long-needed break from writing for a while, traveling with Kenneth.

Jake and Meg's mom is doing much, much better. Between therapy and new meds, she's feeling more emotionally balanced and has worked super hard on her rapport with Jake and Meg, and is even pretty good with Callie, although she's not quite there yet- can't say I blame her.

Mr. Hansen, aka Samuel, is engaged and plans to marry Christy the summer after our junior year of college. Christy is a gem! She's been such a wonderful addition to their family—thankfully!

Christy and Callie ended up moving to our Texas town since Christy and Samuel are engaged, making it all much easier on everyone. Callie has meshed right in with Jake, Meg, Beth, and me. We are all so glad that she is an amazing person and not an evil stepsister to be!!

My birthday is on August 14, and guess what happened on my birthday weekend? Jake had apparently been planning this for months, and everyone knew, except *me*. He totally surprised me and asked me to marry him, and I said yes, of course. We got engaged and plan to get married after we graduate from UT Austin.

Wanna know HOW Jake proposed to me? Let me tell you! It was the weekend after Zac and Sarah's wedding! Woohee!! What a crazy, busy, but awesome wedding weekend THAT was! So, needless to say, we were all looking forward to spending the upcoming weekend doing hardly anything! So, Jake and I slept in on Saturday. It was my birthday, August 14th, and we had already ended our summer jobs since we were leaving the next weekend for UT Austin. Jake said he thought we could go for a walk later in the evening- when the sun had gone down, even though the heat would still be there, but that sounded great to me. We both hung out at our own houses until Jake texted me, as he was coming over to my house with Meg and Callie in tow to hang out with Beth.

Jake <hey you! Just pulling up. Are you ready to go for a walk?>

Gracie <yeah sure I'm going to change quickly then I'll come out>

I ran upstairs to put on my fave yellow sundress and sandals. I'd been hanging in shorts and a tee, so I spruced myself up a bit. Pulled my hair into a messy bun and swiped my lips with lip gloss.

I did a once-over glance at myself in my long mirror.

Okay, not too bad. Off I go!

I walk down the steps and call to mom to tell her that Jake and I are going to take a walk, then probs be back to chill and watch a movie.

"Mom!! I'm going on a walk with Jake. Be back soon!" Mom pops her head out of the kitchen.

"Okay! Have fun. See you two soon!" Mom gives me a goofy smile.

Okay, what was that? My mom is so silly sometimes!

I open the front door, and I see Jake leaning against his Rubicon.

Is it just me, or does Jake look even more fine than he usually does???

"Hey, Gracie! Ah, you look so pretty!"

"Aw, thanks, Jake. You look really good yourself!" We embrace in a gentle hug. And Jake kisses me on my awaiting lips. Then he takes my hand, and we start walking to what I assume is our little park and our favorite spot, near my house.

"How was your day today?" Jake asks me as we slowly walk out of my driveway and onto the sidewalk.

"So chill. I loved it! What about you?" I ask him in return.

"Same! It was so relaxing to do absolutely nothing!!" He smiles at me.

"Oh my GOSH I know! I was literally exhausted and just needed to do nada." I smile back at him.

We continue to hold hands, but we fall into a comfortable silence. We are almost to the playground area, and I let go of Jake's hand so I can sprint to the swing. He does the same. We laugh and swing, laughing some more for about 30 minutes or so. It is so freeing! I love this boy so much because we can do simple and silly things like swing and laugh, and be perfectly content. Jake slows his swing down. I follow suit. We drag our feet until we've come to a complete stop. Jake turns to me, and his face is serious. Not sad, or angry, but a sincere, serious look.

"You good, Jake?" I ask him.

"I am more than good, Gracie. I'm terrific and I am very much in love with you and want to ask you if you'll marry me when we graduate from UT Austin?" He gets down off of the swing and kneels in front of me, and pulls a little bag out of his pocket.

"Holy! What? Of course! Yes! Oh myyyyy stars!! Jake! I love you so much!!" I say smiling ear to ear, like that Cheshire cat in Alice in Wonderland.

Jake pulls out the most beautiful rectangle-shaped diamond ring in white gold.

He takes my left hand and carefully pushes the ring onto my left hand ring finger.

"Oh my gosh! It's gorgeous!" Jake rises and cups my face into his hands and kisses me gently.

"I wanted to tell you I love you when we got engaged because I wanted to make sure I was careful about using those magical words at the right time," Jake says sweetly.

"Oh, Jake. I've wanted to tell you I love you for so many days, but today is THE day, and wow! I love you so so much! And I can't wait to be married to you forever!"

We kiss again, and then I bring my hand up to admire my ring.

"It's seriously breathtaking! I literally love it!!" I grin at him and give him a huge hug.

"Shall we go back and tell everyone?" Jake asks me with a smile.

"Absolutely!!" I say with sheer happiness.

Jake takes my hand again, and we walk quickly until we arrive at my house. Jake opens the front door and lets me into my home, and we both walk into the kitchen, where, unbeknownst to me, everyone from both of our families is waiting for us!

I put out my left hand and show everyone! Jake has his arm around my waist, and then there are squeals of delight, so many hugs and cheek kisses, and congratulations! I am beaming. Jake is, too, and we revel in these precious moments for a very long time.

And me? I can't help but keep looking at my ring for the entire evening, and each time I am in absolute awe. I love and adore it. It's perfect! I'm so happy! I sneak peeks at Jake because we end up talking to different family members and are no longer together, and he does the same. Every time he looks at me, I feel a warm sensation travel throughout my entire body! It feels like I'm being warmed by the sun. I feel so happy!!

Like I can't even put into words how happy I feel! If I were to describe how I think in colors, it would be a bright yellow with pinks and purples mixed into it like a summer sunset! Warmth. Happiness. Satisfaction and utter contentment. The only thought that niggles in my brain is that I sure wish my dad was here to see Jake and me together, but I think I know that he's been looking down from heaven since he's been gone, and smiling about Jake and me!

ALSO BY KARY JANE HUTTO